The Secret of the Old Sleigh

Other Linda Craig® Mysteries in Armada

LINDA CRAIG®

The Secret of the Old Sleigh

ANN SHELDON

Illustrated by St Ward

Armada

First published in the U.S.A. in 1983
by Wanderer Books,
A Simon & Schuster Division of Gulf & Western Corporation.
First published in the U.K. in Armada in 1983 by
Fontana Paperbacks, 8 Grafton Street, London W1X 3LA

Printed in Great Britain by
William Collins Sons & Co. Ltd, Glasgow

Contents

Linda drove Chica in the gleaming sleigh . . .

Glossary

Adobe   Sun-dried bricks used for building in California, Mexico and Arizona.

Burlap   A coarse-textured cloth made of jute, flax or hemp.

Careen   To tilt or swerve at speed.

Chili   Shortening of "chili con carne" — a hot, spicy Mexican stew made of chili-flavoured minced beef.

Corral   A pen for cattle or horses.

Doorjamb   One of the two vertical posts each side of a door frame.

Saddlehorn   The pommel of a western saddle round which a lasso can be looped.

Upgrade   A slope upwards.

Wagon tongue   The harnessing pole of a vehicle.

A Valuable Find   1

"You know we've got just three days to decide what kind of parade unit we're going to enter in the Christmas Parade," Bob Craig told his sixteen-year-old sister Linda as they sat on the corral fence watching Linda's palomino filly Chica d'Oro rolling in the dust.

Linda sighed, pushing back her long, black hair, her dark eyes meeting her brother's. "I was thinking that it might be fun to drive Chica in the parade," she said. "I mean, if we could find an unusual vehicle to hitch her to."

Bob laughed. At eighteen, he was tall and sandy-haired, his face lightly dotted with freckles, very different from his Spanish-looking sister. "You just want to show off Chica's new talents," he teased.

"Well, she does drive beautifully," Linda admitted, "but it's for Kathy's sake, too. Since her horse was sick last week, she won't be able to ride Patches in the parade. If we use Chica and some sort of wagon, Kathy and Larry can ride in it with us."

"What's all this?" Bronco Mallory, Bob and Linda's grandfather, joined them at the corral.

"Linda just suggested that we drive instead of ride in the Christmas Parade," Bob told him. "What do you think?"

"Well, you've trained Chica nicely, Linda, and it would be different to have the Rancho del Sol entry be a wagon of some sort. Have you looked in the old shed to see if there's anything in there you could fix up and use?"

"Let's look now," Linda suggested.

The shed was beyond the complex of corrals and barns that served the ranch, and the door creaked as if in protest when Bronco pulled it open. Dust filled the air and there were spiderwebs glinting on all the surfaces. "I guess it's been a while since anyone has been interested in using an old wagon or buggy," Bronco observed wryly.

"I didn't know you had so many," Linda murmured, squinting after the brightness of the winter sun. She and her brother had come to California to live permanently with their grandparents at Rancho del Sol after their parents had been killed in a car accident.

"Well, just what do you have in mind?" Bronco asked, moving into the shadowy interior and uncovering the first old wagon.

"I don't know," Linda admitted, going past him into the rear of the building, her eye suddenly caught by an unusual shape in the corner farthest from the door. She gasped as she pulled a piece of old canvas off the vehicle.

"Find something, Sis?" Bob asked.

"Oh, look!" Linda called. "It's just perfect."

"Let's get it out where we can see it," Bronco suggested, moving a small buggy clear of the way and grasping one of the shafts that extended from the shadowed vehicle. "Give me a hand, Bob, this is a heavy one."

Linda moved a wagon tongue out of their path while the two men grunted and groaned as they dragged the bulky vehicle outside. Only then did they both step back and look. Bob burst out laughing. "A sleigh, Linda?" he asked. "In California?"

"Oh, dear!" Linda complained. "I didn't realize . . . I mean, it's so beautiful and with the two seats, I just thought how perfect it would be for the four of us. I'm sorry you worked so hard dragging it out."

"I was wondering why anything with wheels would be so heavy," Bob commented. "It is a shame, though. A sleigh would be really appropriate for the season."

"If we put bells on Chica's harness, and holly and mistletoe on the sleigh . . ." Linda stopped speaking as her eyes rested on the sturdy runners that supported the beautifully carved wooden sleigh.

"You'd need a team of six big mules to pull that thing down the street," Bob told her. "It must weigh a ton." He sighed. "And now we have to put it back inside."

"Wait a minute," Bronco cautioned. "Maybe there is a way you could use it."

Linda looked at her grandfather doubtfully as Bob bent to examine the runners.

"There's no way we could take those runners off," Bob reported. "This wasn't built to be a convertible."

Bronco chuckled. "I was thinking more about that rolling platform we used to transport adobe bricks last year. Don't you think the sleigh would fit on it?"

Bob studied it for a moment, then nodded. "The runners might stick out at the back a little, but other than that . . ."

"Would it work?" Linda asked. "I mean, could Chica pull it all right on the platform?"

"The platform is low enough that the shafts should be right," Bronco said, circling the sleigh. "I'd say that it would be fine once that sleigh is cleaned and polished. Do you want to use it? No doubt, it will take a lot more work than a buggy or wagon would."

Linda looked up at her brother. He shrugged. "It's up to you, Sis," he told her. "You'll be the one doing most of the work, since I have to be in town tomorrow."

"Yes, I think it will be perfect," Linda said. "I'll ask Luisa for something to polish the wood, and once I get all the dust out of the seat cushions, it will look fine." She was already on her way to the kitchen to ask the Mexican housekeeper for cleaning supplies, her mind full of ideas as to what she could wear as she drove the golden filly down the streets of town. The group would surely attract plenty of attention, and they just might win the trophy for having the entry with the most holiday spirit in the parade.

Once she began wiping the dust and dirt from the graceful swan necks that rose at the front of the sleigh, Linda was intrigued by the beauty of the carving. The swans' perfectly sculptured wings enclosed the two padded seats, and on the front boards connecting the two graceful heads and forming the front of the sleigh was carved a peaceful scene of swans floating on a lily-pad-dotted pool.

Since Bob and Bronco had disappeared to discuss ways of mounting the sleigh on the wheeled platform, Linda opened the corral gate so that Chica could come and keep her company while she worked on the sleigh. "So what do you think of it?" she asked as the filly's gold and white nose sniffed delicately at this new contraption.

Chica's intelligent brown eyes looked at Linda, her golden ears pricked forward to listen to her words as she moved on around the sleigh. The filly sniffed first the dingy red cushions padding the two seats, then the long runners extending beyond the sleek wingsides that ended in carefully executed feather tips.

"Think you'd like to wear a belled harness and pull us in the parade?" Linda asked, putting down the dust cloth and taking time to follow the filly around the sleigh. To her surprise, she found that even the boards that enclosed the rear of the sleigh were covered with a carved scene, this one of a lake with skaters on its frozen surface.

"I can't believe the work on this sleigh," Linda observed as she stepped over one of the runners to study the carving on the panel below the seat cushions. She picked up her cloth to clean away the thick collection of cobwebs that obscured the design.

The cloth was soft, so that it slipped in well around the intricate carving. But as she moved it along the surface, the cloth snagged. Linda tugged gently, but it didn't come loose. Afraid of pulling out a splinter and ruining a part of the design, she got down on her hands and knees and began carefully freeing the fabric, her fingers seeking the rough spot in the carving.

A loud *click* startled Linda, and Chica's snort told her it had startled the filly, too. The cloth pulled away from Linda's fingers as a part of the panel separated from the rest and swung open.

"A secret panel," Linda exclaimed, delighted. "What in the world . . .?"

"What are you doing, Sis?" Bob asked suddenly. She had been so surprised by her find that she hadn't noticed his approach.

"I've found a secret compartment in the sleigh," Linda answered excitedly. "Look!"

"Hey, that's really something." Bob joined her in the narrow front of the vehicle, peering into the dark recess under the seat. "What's that inside?" he asked, sliding a hand cautiously into the compartment.

"I was just going to look," Linda told him, caught between annoyance at his being first to explore the hidden area she'd discovered and gratitude that she didn't have to reach into what might be a hideout for all sorts of spiders and other crawling creatures.

"Feels like some kind of book," Bob said, producing a very battered-looking notebook, which he handed to Linda. "There's something else, too," he continued, reaching back into the recess. "It's not a big hiding place, and I brushed something . . ."

Linda held the notebook carefully, feeling the fragility of the old cover as she carefully brushed away the dust. There was writing on the faded cover, but it was too washed-out to read in the bright sunlight. She opened the book.

"Journal of Melanie Davis," fine handwriting announced on the first page. Beneath the title was a date nearly seventy years old.

"It's some kind of diary!" Linda exclaimed. "Bob, do you think it could have been in there for seventy years?"

Bob shrugged. "Bronco says the sleigh is around one hundred years old, so I guess it could." He handed her something else. "What do you think this is?" he asked.

Linda put the book down on the seat cushion and looked at the object he'd handed her. At first glance, it appeared to be just a small black stone. But on closer examination, she could see that the upper end, where it narrowed almost to a point, had been pierced by a hole. Also, the surface of the stone was rough, and when she cleaned it with her rag, she could see that some kind of design or pattern had been carved into the shiny black surface.

"Well," Bob asked, "what do you think it is?"

"Maybe some kind of good-luck piece," Linda suggested. "I expect that hole in the top means it could be worn on a chain or leather thong." She shrugged. "Maybe there's something about it in the journal."

Bob opened the notebook and read the legend on the title page. "Melanie Davis," he mused. "Do you remember an ancestor by that name?"

Linda shook her head. "I think we should take these in and show them to Doña," she said. "She will know." Their grandmother Rosalinda, a handsome Spanish lady whom Linda resembled and had been named after, was Doña to both the youngsters.

"Don't close that panel till we figure out how it works," Bob warned.

"I already know," Linda answered. "There's a little lever hidden under the carving of the flying swan. See it?" She turned the panel so the sun penetrated the intricate carving. "My dust rag must have caught on it, or maybe I released it when I was trying to get the fabric loose without pulling any splinters off."

"Put Chica in the corral and let's go see what Bronco and Doña know about this," Bob said, opening and closing the panel to test it.

"Oh, wouldn't it be exciting to find out about some mysterious ancestor who owned this sleigh?" Linda murmured as she called the filly from her grazing and put her in the corral.

"I sure don't remember any Davises," Bob said as they hurried towards the handsome Spanish-style house where Doña and Bronco were standing on the porch watching them.

"Did you find something in the sleigh?" Bronco asked as they stepped into the shady area.

Bob and Linda explained quickly while Bronco and Doña examined the notebook and the black stone. Linda finished, "So was Melanie Davis an ancestor?"

Doña shook her head. "Not one of ours, I'm afraid," she replied. "In fact, we were just talking about the sleigh, trying to remember where it came from."

Bronco laughed. "We don't exactly have a lot of use for a sleigh here in the desert."

"So where did it come from?" Bob asked.

"It belonged to a friend of your mother's," Doña answered. "Her name was Olga White. She and her parents lived north of here in the mountains. John and Beatrice White. We still hear from them every year at Christmas. Anyway, Olga and your mother used the sleigh on a visit to a ski resort one holiday season. The Whites didn't have a place to store the sleigh, so we brought it back here, and I guess it's been in the shed ever since."

"You mean the sleigh and the journal belong to someone else?" Linda felt a quick pang of disappointment.

Doña nodded. "I'm afraid so."

"Do you think they'd want them back?" Bob asked.

Bronco laughed. "Not before the parade, I'm sure," he soothed. "Let me get their Christmas card. As I remember, there was a letter with it."

Doña stroked the notebook with gentle fingers. "I have a feeling Beatrice will be very excited about your discovery," she said. "Melanie Davis must be a relative of hers."

16

"Well, I . . ." Linda began, then stopped as she saw her grandfather's face when he emerged from the house. "What is it?" she asked.

"It looks like we have a bit of a coincidence here," Bronco said, handing the letter to Linda. "Read that last paragraph."

Linda scanned the page, then began reading aloud:

Actually, Roz, things haven't been all that good for us this Christmas. You see, we've had a strange burglary. Someone stole Grandpa's carving "The Old Sleigh". (Remember the beautiful wall hanging we had in the den when we lived north of you?) Anyway, it disappeared from our home. Oddly enough, nothing else was taken.

There was more on the other side, but when Linda paused, she could see that her grandmother was frowning. "That is weird," Linda murmured. "I mean, our finding a sleigh here and them losing one up there."

"Where do they live?" Bob asked.

"Near Glacier Park in northern Montana," Bronco answered. "And it is more than strange. I remember that carving, and now that I think about it, I'm sure it was a carved portrait of the sleigh we just brought out of the shed."

"A portrait of the sleigh?" Linda frowned.

"It was a family heirloom," Bronco continued. "John had it appraised for insurance purposes and it was extremely valuable. Beatrice's grandfather was a famous artist, which makes me wonder about the sleigh. We may have been storing something of

17

considerable value out in that old shed without even realizing it."

"But if the sleigh's so valuable, why would the Whites leave it here?" Linda asked. "Besides, they'd have much more use for it in Montana, I'm sure."

Everyone laughed in agreement.

"Why don't we call John and Beatrice and ask them?" Doña suggested with a smile. "If the sleigh is truly that valuable, we should ask their permission before you fix it up to use in the parade, don't you think?"

Linda nodded, crossing her fingers behind her back. Now that she'd seen the sleigh, she was more anxious than ever to use it. It was the perfect entry. "Will you call her for us, Doña?" Linda asked. "Tell her we'll be very careful with the sleigh."

"I will, dear, and I'm sure she'll be very happy that you found these." She picked up the notebook and the black stone and carried them inside with her.

Linda stared after her for a moment, longing to listen in on her grandmother's side of the conversation, but at the same time too restless. "I guess I'll go work on the sleigh some more," she said after a moment. "It needs to be cleaned up whether we use it or not."

"Hoping to find more hidden panels?" Bronco teased.

"You never know," Linda answered.

She was just ready to get into the sleigh again when Bronco's shout called her back to the house. Doña was waiting for her, a strange expression on her face.

"What is it?" Linda asked.

"Beatrice has a proposal for all of us," Doña answered, sinking down in her chair, "and it is something we'll have to decide right away."

Unexpected Visitors   2

"They want us to go to Montana?" Linda shook her head, unable to believe her ears.

"Beatrice even invited Chica, Rocket, and Rango." Doña smiled. "I've told her so much about all of you and she knew your mother so well . . ." She let her words trail off.

"You really think we could go?" Bob asked. "It's so far. It would take us a long time to drive, and with the weather being so uncertain—"

"Ah, you haven't heard the best part," Bronco interrupted. "John would provide round-trip transportation when he comes by for the sleigh."

"When he *what*?" Linda looked from Bronco to Doña and back again.

"John is flying a cargo of Arabian horses to Mexico for a California breeder," Doña explained. "He has a charter cargo service, though he's more or less retired now. Anyway, he'll come back this way and pick all of us up the day after Christmas. Since the plane will be rigged to carry horses, there's no reason to leave Chica and Rocket behind. So what do you think?"

"They've heard about your success at solving mysteries, Linda," Bronco added before the two young people could speak, "and they were rather hoping you'd be able to find out who stole the sleigh carving and why."

"Oh, I'd love to try," Linda admitted, looking at

her brother. "What do you think, Bob? Would you like to go?"

"It sounds terrific," Bob agreed. "Maybe we could even use the sleigh on real snow up there."

"Speaking of using the sleigh, what did Mrs White say about that?" Linda asked quickly.

"You have permission to use it," Doña answered. "She was very pleased to know that it was still in existence. I guess they never realized that it was here. Beatrice said that she had assumed it was destroyed in a barn fire twenty years ago. She cried when I told her we'd found it."

"What about the journal?" Bob asked.

"She's very anxious to read it," Doña told him. "Melanie Davis was her aunt, and according to Beatrice she was the family lady of mystery. No one ever knew what happened to her."

"Another mystery," Linda murmured, intrigued by everything connected with the sleigh.

"I'll call Beatrice back and tell her that we accept her invitation," Doña said.

"And I'll go work on the sleigh," Linda announced happily. "I want to fix it up so it looks just like new."

"And I'll go look in that big trunk in the tack room," Bob offered. "I think I remember seeing a fancy red harness in there."

"One with bells?" Linda asked.

He shrugged. "If it doesn't have bells, I'll get some when I go into town tomorrow."

"Oh, this is going to be so much fun!" Linda giggled. "Just wait till I tell Kathy."

"Why don't you call her later," Doña suggested. "Maybe she'd like to come over and help you clean up the sleigh."

The next few days flew by. Linda and Bob worked on the sleigh and got ready for Christmas and the trip that would follow the celebration. Heavy clothing had to be selected and packed, and other arrangements made.

The day of the parade dawned cold and windy. Their fur-trimmed parkas and the slightly moth-eaten bearskin lap robe felt good as they sat in the parking lot posing for pictures and waiting for the judges to make their selections before the parade began.

Linda was proud of the gleaming sleigh with the puffs of cotton snow moulded around the runners to make it look authentic and to hide the platform it rested on. Chica snorted and danced in place, plainly enjoying the music that came from the bells on her bright red harness.

"Think we'll win the trophy?" honey-blonde Kathy Hamilton asked from the backseat where she sat beside Bob.

"I don't see how you can miss," tall, sun-bronzed Larry Spencer observed from his seat alongside Linda. "There's nothing to compare with this in the parade."

"I know the Whites will be thrilled if we do," Linda admitted, adjusting the wreaths of holly and mistletoe that they'd strung along both sides of the vehicle. "They're very proud of this sleigh."

"Everyone is interested," Kathy observed. "That man in the brown plaid coat has been staring at it ever since we got here."

"Maybe he likes antiques," Bob suggested.

"I think we're going to find out," Larry said. "He's coming over."

The man stepped up to the side of the sleigh,

smiling to reveal a lot of very white teeth. "I would like to make an offer for this sleigh," he said, his voice cold and his eyes hidden by the lenses of his dark glasses.

"I'm sorry, sir, the sleigh isn't for sale," Linda told him, tightening her hold on the reins as Chica bounced forward a few strides.

"But I would be willing to pay a great deal of money for it," the man continued, following them. "I'm a collector of antique vehicles and I'd like to add this one to my collection."

"I'm sorry, sir . . ." Linda began.

"You haven't heard my offer." The smile still twisted the man's lips, but Linda could hear the anger in his tone and she was sure that the glasses hid mean eyes.

"The sleigh isn't mine to sell," Linda replied, and to her relief one of the parade officials came over to wave them into line.

"I'll need the owner's name," the man called after them, but Linda didn't look back. She had a strange feeling the man wasn't what he claimed to be.

Band music blared around them and the mounted flag bearers rode into the street to the cheers of the crowd. Riding groups, marching troops, floats, and more bands began to move. The parade was under way.

A loudspeaker crackled and shrilled as they reached the street, but the wind was blowing very hard and there was too much noise for Linda to make out what was being said. Laughing gaily, she waved to the judges and the crowd, proud to be in the sleigh and suddenly very excited about the trip they would be making in just one more day.

"We won!" Bob shouted.

"Already? How do you know?" Linda asked, looking around.

"The judges just announced it," Bob answered. "We took the trophy for best float."

The rest of the day passed in a blur of photographs and interviews as all the winners were assembled after the parade and the trophies were presented. Then it was back to the ranch for a Christmas Eve party, with Kathy, Larry, and their families all joining in the festivities.

Christmas Day brought the fiesta with the ranch hands and other employees of the Rancho del Sol, and by mid-afternoon Linda was dizzy from all the food, music, and dancing. She left the party, which was being held outside in the sunshine, and went into the house. The phone was ringing and she answered it with a sigh.

"Is this the Mallory residence?" a slightly familiar voice inquired.

"Yes, it is," Linda replied, frowning as she tried to remember where she'd heard the voice before.

"I'm calling about the sleigh that was pictured in the paper today," the voice continued.

Linda said nothing, realizing that she'd heard the voice at the parade and that it belonged to the man who'd wanted to buy the sleigh.

"I represent a collector who is very interested in purchasing the sleigh, and I wonder if I might come by and discuss it with the owner?" the man continued after a momentary pause.

"I'm sorry, but the sleigh is not for sale," Linda told him firmly.

"Everything is for sale, miss," the voice told her coldly. "Now let me talk to the owner."

"The owner isn't here," Linda answered. "If you

23

want to make an offer, I suggest you write to John White at Lakeville, Montana; but I really don't think . . .." She stopped, realizing that she was talking to herself. The caller had hung up on her.

"Thank you, too," she muttered into the receiver.

"Trouble, Linda?" Doña asked, making her start.

"Just a man calling about the sleigh," Linda replied. "He was admiring it at the parade yesterday and he wanted to buy it."

"Beatrice would never sell it," Doña stated flatly.

"I tried to tell him that it wasn't for sale, but I don't think he believed me."

"Well, Beatrice and John will set him straight if he contacts them. Meantime, the party is almost over, so I think you should come back outside."

Once the party ended, Linda finished her packing, then slipped out in the quiet evening to go down to spend a few minutes with Chica. Rango, the half-shepherd, half-coyote dog, followed her. Yawning and stretching as he trotted along, he wagged his feathery yellow-tan tail happily.

Chica and Rocket stood in the corral. They had been left outside in the cool air to help them adjust to the much colder weather that awaited them in Montana. Chica neighed a greeting and came over to nuzzle Linda.

Linda scratched both horse and dog. "Just think," she told them, "tomorrow you'll be seeing snow for the very first time. I wonder what you will do."

Chica rubbed her head against Linda, and Rango offered a paw. "At least the Whites have a nice warm stable for you," Linda went on, talking because she knew that both her horse and dog were soothed by the sound of her voice. "So you won't freeze. But if we go riding or take the sleigh out, you'll feel it."

Her mind went to the sleigh, which was now carefully wrapped in padded canvas mats and resting in the front half of the big horse trailer. They would use the vehicle to transport the sleigh and the horses to the airport in the morning. She sighed, thinking of the parties she'd miss here, and the fun with Larry and Kathy.

But there was the curious journal, and the disappearance of the carving of the sleigh. She pushed back her hair, which the wind was blowing in her eyes. She'd been so busy getting ready for the parade and the trip to Montana that she had barely even had a chance to think about the journal, and Doña had said there was a mystery about Melanie Davis, too.

"I hope Mrs White will let me read the journal," she confided to the horses and Rango. "I'd love to learn more about life so long ago and maybe find out what happened to Melanie and why the journal was in the sleigh." She stopped, yawning, suddenly exhausted after the long, busy days. It was time to go to bed, since they would be leaving before dawn to meet Mr White at the airport.

In her room, she admired her Christmas gifts, taking out the slender gold chain that had been Bob's present. It would be pretty alone or with one of the delicate gold charms she'd collected through the years.

Thinking that she might wear it tomorrow, she moved to her jewellery box and lifted the lid. Then sh remembered the strange black stone that had been in the hidden compartment. Curious, she got it from her suitcase and slipped the chain through the hole. Once it was around her neck, she looked in the mirror and smiled. The fragile gold chain with the small dark stone had a striking and mysterious effect against her smooth skin.

Pleased with herself, she got into bed and closed her eyes, relaxing into sleep almost at once, the stone warm against her throat. Dreams of sleighs and snow and laughing faces took over immediately.

At first, the barking seemed a part of the dream. Then slowly she realized that it wasn't. Sleepily, she sat up. It was Rango, and he sounded as though he meant business! Linda picked up her dressing gown, and shoving her feet into her slippers, she hurried through the silent house.

It was very dark outside. The wind had dropped and clouds covered the moon and stars. She followed the sounds of Rango's barking towards the old shed, her heartbeat quickening as she saw a large truck beside the building. Suddenly Rango's bark became a yelp. Then there was silence.

Frightened for the dog, Linda ran over the rough ground and into the shadows of the building, not sure what she was going to do, but ready to fight to protect the brave dog.

"I tell you, it's not in here," a man's voice said, making her gasp since it seemed to come from right beside her.

"It has to be," a second male voice snapped as she stopped just outside the shed door. "I already looked in the barn and there's nothing there but a big old horse trailer."

"Well, they must have taken it somewhere." The man sighed. "What did you do with the dog?"

"I dropped a burlap bag over his head and tied it to his collar," the second man said with a chuckle. "I was waiting when he stuck his head in here."

Linda heard a scuffling noise, and a big body plunged against her legs. Sure that it was the confused and frightened dog, she dropped down beside him and put her arms around his struggling body, trying to reassure him without speaking.

"Hey, there are lights coming on in the house," the first man said. "We'd better get out of here."

"The boss ain't going to like it that we didn't get it," the second man said.

"I don't . . ."

Linda was trying to drag Rango away from the open shed door, but it was too late. The men came through and saw her. For just a moment, they simply stared. Then one of them reached out, grabbed both her and Rango, and threw them into the blackness of the shed. The door slammed behind them. She crashed into something solid and went down, the furious dog on top of her.

Masked Attacker

It was several minutes before the shed door crashed open and Bronco came in, the glare of the flashlight he carried blinding Linda. He dropped to his knees beside her as Cactus Mac, the ranch's foreman, freed Rango from the tangled burlap bag.

"What happened, Linda?" Bronco gasped. "Are you all right?"

Linda sat up carefully, aware of a throbbing in the back of her head where she'd struck it on one of the wagons and already feeling some bruises from her stumbling fall. "I'm not hurt," she told the two men, then looked around. "Did they get away?" she asked.

"Who?" Bronco inquired.

"There were two men in here." She explained how she'd come out, then paused to hug Rango as he came to assure himself that she was safe.

Bronco and Cactus Mac exchanged glances. "I thought I heard a truck leaving," the foreman said. "Didn't see it, though."

"What were they doing over here?" Bronco asked as he helped Linda to her feet.

"Looking for the sleigh, I think," Linda replied, then repeated what she'd heard them say. "I guess they didn't bother to look in the horse trailer," she finished, "so they didn't see it."

"Sounds like we were wise to load it last night," Bronco observed. "But I wonder who—"

"The man from the parade," Linda broke in. "He called yesterday and was very insistent about wanting to buy it, so he might be the one."

Bronco sighed. "I'm afraid we don't have any proof of that, Linda," he cautioned her. "Buying the sleigh is one thing, but stealing it is quite something else."

"Just as well you're taking it away from here tomorrow," Cactus Mac said. "If they come looking while you're gone, they'll be disappointed."

"Are you sure you'll be all right, Linda?" Bronco asked.

"I'll have a few bruises," Linda replied. "I should be fine in the morning."

Bronco looked as though he might like to argue, but after instructing Cactus Mac to post a guard for the rest of the night, he followed Linda back to the house. After making sure her bruises were not serious, he allowed her to go back to bed.

Though she was tired, Linda had trouble falling asleep, for her mind was filled with questions. Rare and beautiful as the sleigh was, she wondered if any collector would resort to theft to get it, since it was one of a kind and would be simple to identify. But what other reason could there be for stealing the sleigh? She winced as she turned over, remembering that another carving had already been taken—the wall hanging that Bronco said was a picture of the swan sleigh.

She squirmed to another position and felt the weight of the black stone pulling lightly against the chain. Perhaps tomorrow she would learn all the secrets of the journal and the stone. Till then, she'd just have to wait. She slept without dreams till the alarm woke her before dawn.

* * *

29

John White's plane was a surprise. A half-dozen high-sided stalls had been constructed for his cargo to Mexico, and there were a number of large crates carefully secured in the rear and on each side of the plane.

"Put the horses in the two front stalls," John instructed, "and make sure that they're tied securely. There's nothing more dangerous than a terrified horse loose in a plane."

"We'll stay with them," Linda assured him, stroking Chica's neck as they waited for the men to load the sleigh.

"You'll have to be in your seats for takeoff," John warned her with a smile. "We have seatbelt rules just like the airlines. Once we're in flight, however, you're free to wander about as much as you like. Anyone who is interested can come up to the cockpit and see how easy this thing is to fly."

"I'll be there," Bob assured him.

"Do we have to put Rango in a crate?" Doña asked, patting the excited dog.

"No, just keep him beside you during takeoff and landing." John scratched behind the golden-tan ears. "I like dogs, but not in the cockpit."

Rango waved his big tail, then went over to stand beside the horses.

Chica and Rocket, used to travelling, were easy to load into the plane, but once the motors were started and the aircraft began to move along the runway, gathering speed for takeoff, Linda could hear them snorting and stamping their feet. As soon as they were safely off the ground, she unbuckled her seatbelt and hurried back to the two stalls.

The horses were loaded into the plane . . .

31

Rocket's eyes were rolling and Chica's ears were flipping rapidly as she tossed her head, pulling against the stout tie rope. "Hey, you two," Linda greeted them, putting a hand on each one's head. "There's nothing to be afraid of. We're just in a different kind of trailer and I'm right here with you."

Rocket fought her touch for a moment, then calmed down. Chica responded even more quickly, rubbing her head against Linda's shoulder. Linda stayed with them, talking quietly, aware that the words were unimportant. It was her tone that would soothe them.

It was a long flight, but fairly smooth. They stopped once for refuelling and lunch at an airport coffee shop. The horses were unloaded and allowed to trot around on long lines, snorting and bucking a little in the unaccustomed coldness of the northern air. On the second takeoff, they were so busy munching at a few wisps of hay that they didn't even snort or fuss.

"Seasoned travellers already," Bronco observed with a chuckle as he helped Linda check the horses after takeoff. "You'd think they'd been flying everywhere for years."

"They just trust us," Linda murmured, fingering the black stone.

"I see you're wearing your discovery," Bronco said.

Linda nodded. "I wanted to wear my new chain, and the stone was just lying there."

"It looks as though it was meant to be worn," Bronco told her, lifting the stone and running one hard thumb over its surface. "Have you figured out what the marks on it mean?"

"Not really," Linda admitted. "I'm sure it's some kind of design, but even with a magnifying glass I couldn't tell what it was. It was definitely carved in by someone—I mean, they aren't random scratches or anything like that. Maybe Mrs White will know something about it."

"We should be finding out pretty soon," Bronco said. "She'll be meeting us at the Lakeville airport. John says she's terribly anxious to see the sleigh and to read the journal."

"I hope she'll let us read it," Linda confided. "I didn't feel that I had the right to read it after Doña called her and she said that it belonged to her aunt, but . . ."

"You haven't exactly had time to sit down and read, anyway," Bronco reminded her. "Between getting ready for the parade, all our Christmas celebrations, and preparing for this trip."

"And now we're almost there." Linda smiled. "I can hardly wait."

"You just want to build a snowman," he teased. "At least the weather is good. They have a couple of feet of snow, but it has been thawing a little, so the ground is clear in spots and it gets up to forty some days."

"Forty?" Linda swallowed hard. "I think we are going to freeze to death. I feel like a misplaced desert flower all of a sudden."

"You'll adjust, and so will the horses. We'll have to keep them blanketed for a day or two, but they'll grow more hair quickly. They already have a good start." He stroked Rocket's neck.

"Hey, you two, time to strap in," Bob called, emerging from the cockpit where he'd spent almost the entire flight. "Mr White says we'll be landing in about ten minutes."

Linda took her seat as the big plane circled for landing. Her fingers stole to her neck to touch the

33

strange stone and trace the odd marks, trying to understand the pattern that they formed.

The cold air rushed in the moment the side door of the plane opened. Linda got into her parka, then hurried over to back Chica out of the stall. She buckled a heavy red wool blanket in place over the filly's golden body, while Bob put a blue blanket on Rocket. They led them snorting and dancing down the ramp and into the bright Montana sunshine.

Introductions took only a moment and Linda felt the same instant warmth from the small, hazel-eyed Mrs White as she had from her distinguished, grey-haired husband. "I can't tell you how happy I am to meet you at last," Mrs White told her as she accepted the journal from Linda's hands. "And under such happy circumstances, too. Imagine the old sleigh turning up that way, and then to think you were clever enough to find this." Her eyes misted. "It's as though you're giving me a gift of my own past."

"It was just an accident," Linda protested, embarrassed by the woman's words. "I mean, my finding the hidden compartment. And—" She stopped abruptly. "I forgot," she said, reaching up and unclasping the golden chain, "there was more in the compartment. This stone was in with the journal."

"A stone?" Mrs White accepted the stone with a frown. "But what . . . ?"

"There's some carving on it," Linda continued. "I don't know what it means, but it probably belonged to your aunt—if she's the one who put the journal in the sleigh."

Mrs White turned the stone over in her hand, then looked at Linda. "Would you like to keep this?" she asked. "It could be sort of a memento of your discovery."

"Oh, I'd love to have it, but . . ."

"Put it back on, dear," Mrs White urged. "I'm sure Melanie would want you to have it as a reward for bringing this to light and for returning our lovely sleigh."

Linda accepted the stone and slipped it back on the chain, but before she could fasten the clasp, a rather stocky young man stepped forward. "Let me do that," he said, taking the chain out of her hands and nearly dropping the stone on the runway. "I'm Randy Fox," he continued. "Mrs White asked me to ride over and meet you." He gestured towards the big white horse that stood tied to the fence on the far side of the runway.

"Oh, Randy, I'm sorry," Mrs White broke in, making the proper introductions for everyone. "I invited Randy along with the idea that you young people might enjoy riding to the house instead of going in the car," she explained. "It's only about three miles cross-country, and your horses would probably welcome the exercise after being cooped up in those tiny stalls all day."

"I'm your guide," Randy said with a grin that was obviously meant to be friendly, but somehow left Linda feeling cold. "I live just about half a mile beyond the Whites' place."

"That sounds good to me," Bob agreed after a glance at Bronco. "What do you say, Linda?"

"I'm ready," Linda answered.

"Before you saddle up, why don't you two young men help us unload the sleigh?" Bronco suggested. "It is one heavy vehicle."

"Too bad we didn't bring the harness," Linda said. "We could have hitched Chica to the sleigh and all made the trip that way."

"Is that pony Chica?" Randy asked, his tone making the question sound almost mocking.

"She's not a pony," Linda protested.

"She's not very big." Randy walked towards the filly, then stopped when a low growl came from the dog standing beside her. "No wonder she has her own guard dog," he quipped.

"Rango, come here," Linda ordered the coyote-shepherd. "Chica isn't full grown yet," she explained as patiently as she could. "Also, she lost her mother shortly after she was born, so she may be a little smaller because of that."

"She's a pretty colour," Randy acknowledged.

"She's also quite a good show horse," Bronco commented. "Linda has a whole shelf full of trophies from the shows she has been in."

"Oh, a show horse." Randy's tone underlined his lack of interest and he turned away to follow John White into the plane.

Linda cast an exasperated glance at Doña, then giggled as her grandmother gave her a consoling wink. It was obvious that talking about Chica d'Oro wasn't going to impress Randy, but she was sure that once he saw Chica in action, he'd have to change his mind.

"Why don't I saddle the horses," she suggested. "Then we can be on our way as soon as the sleigh is unloaded from the plane." She found herself shivering in the cold air and was glad to be moving around to get warm, though she hated taking the blankets off the horses, fearing they would be cold, too.

Once they set off, however, it was plain that the horses were enjoying the crisp air and the white carpet under their hooves. They danced and snorted, bounding as the cold snow touched their legs, then settling down to a more sedate pace once they joined Randy and his quiet mount.

"This is really beautiful," Linda murmured, her eyes feasting on the vistas of forests and snow-covered mountains that rose in all directions. "I didn't know it would be like this."

Randy reined his heavy horse close to Chica. "So tell me how you happened to discover the secret compartment in the sleigh," he said.

Linda swallowed a sigh, but gave him a friendly answer, sure that he was asking because he wanted to make up for his rather rude words earlier. He was not, however, content with her answers, and continued to ask questions as they rode across snow-covered fields and into the forest that grew near the lake.

Finally, in self-defence, she reined Chica away from the bigger horse and looked back over her shoulder. It was then that she heard the drone of a motor and saw a flash of bright yellow between the trees.

"Hey, there's a snowmobile, Bob," she called to her brother, who was riding ahead of her.

Bob reined in and stood in his stirrups, peering into the trees. "I don't see it," he said, "but I noticed one when we left the airport. It was on the crest of the hill on the far side, and someone was watching us."

"I didn't notice," Linda admitted.

Bob grinned. "You probably couldn't see the snowmobile, as it was on the other side of the plane. I didn't notice till I was climbing out of the trailer after we loaded the sleigh. I just happened to look in that direction and I was high enough to see him."

"Why would someone be watching us?" Linda asked.

Bob shrugged. "Maybe there's not much excitement around here."

Linda giggled. "Why don't we split up and ride back a little way to see if someone is following us?" she suggested.

"Are you thinking what I am?" Bob asked.

"Someone was sure after the sleigh last night," Linda admitted.

"But we don't have the sleigh with us," Bob reminded her.

"I guess it doesn't make much sense," Linda agreed with a sigh. "But I just have a funny feeling that something is going on."

"Are you two having a private conference?" Randy asked, riding so close that Chica moved away from the bigger horse, her ears back.

"We were just wondering who was riding the yellow snowmobile," Linda said quickly. "Do you know?"

Randy looked around. "I don't see anyone," he answered, his cold eyes coming back to mock her again. "Are you sure you didn't imagine it?"

"I heard the motor and saw it through the trees over there," Linda replied, keeping her tone polite with an effort.

"You think someone is trying to follow you?" Randy asked sarcastically. "Maybe steal that fancy golden horse?" His laughter was like a slap. "Come on," he called over his shoulder, "you don't want to be late for your welcome party."

Linda looked at her brother, seeing the same anger and confusion that she was feeling reflected in his face. He shrugged, then touched his heels to

The view below them was like a painting . . .

Rocket's sides. "What party?" he asked, catching up to Randy.

Linda urged Chica after them, but she continued to look over her shoulder, sure that she heard the snarl of the snowmobile from time to time. This visit isn't exactly getting off to the kind of start I expected, she thought wryly.

The moment they left the shelter of the trees, however, her spirits revived, for what lay below them was like something out of an old painting. A large log house and nearby log barn were nestled beneath the pines, smoke rising from the house's chimney.

Beyond the house was the lakeshore. A bonfire was already blazing there, while nearly a dozen brightly dressed skaters spun around on the frozen lake. "Your welcome party," Randy announced rather ungraciously. "We're all members of the local Saddle Club and we wanted to meet you and invite you to ride with us while you're here."

"That's very nice," Linda said. "And it looks like fun, too. I haven't been skating for a couple of years."

"It's a good thing we brought our skates," Bob agreed. "I just hope we haven't forgotten how." They hurried down the hill, eager to meet everyone.

In spite of her doubts about her skating ability, Linda found herself relaxing as soon as she moved out on the ice. The other members of the Saddle Club were much friendlier than Randy had been. Their compliments about Chica and Rocket warmed her as she skimmed over the ice, feeling the cold air turning her cheeks red and bringing tears to her eyes.

She didn't really notice that she'd left the other skaters behind as she followed the rocky, snow-covered shoreline. Nor did she realize that one skater had come after her. Only when she'd rounded an outcropping of stones did she slow her headlong pace and look back.

The figure hurtled at her, his face covered by a black and green ski mask. For a moment Linda froze with shock. Then she screamed and tried to move out of his path. However, her balance was too precarious, and she found herself crashing to the ice as his hard shoulder struck her.

The figure dropped beside her, and mitten-covered hands fumbled at the neck of her parka, tearing it open. Linda caught her breath and screamed furiously. One mittened hand immediately covered her nose and mouth, smothering her as the other hand tangled in the chain around her neck and began dragging on it.

Linda squirmed and fought, trying to free her mouth to scream again, frightened as the hand kept her from catching her breath. The man mumbled something as he tried to separate her chain from the scarf she'd wound around her neck. Then suddenly he leaped to his feet as an angry shout came from the direction of the bonfire.

Gasping, Linda sat up as Bob came flying around the rocky outcropping. She waved him after the racing skater who'd attacked her. But even as he sped by, she knew that he wasn't going to catch the man. He was already disappearing into the trees, running awkwardly on his skates, but escaping nevertheless.

Bob skidded to a stop at the shoreline, then came skating back to help her to her feet. "Are you all right?" he asked. "What happened?"

"He knocked me down," Linda gasped. "I think he was after the stone." She stripped off a mitten and reached inside her parka to make sure that the small weight still hung on her chain. "He . . ." She stopped as the other skaters came up to them.

"What happened to you?" Randy asked.

"Who was the skater in the green and black ski mask?" Linda inquired, instead of answering.

The other skaters looked at her curiously, then at each other. Finally, a girl named Diane Phelps shrugged and came to Linda's side. "There wasn't anyone in a ski mask, Linda," she said, her green eyes full of concern.

"Well, the man who knocked me down was wearing one," Linda informed them all. "Didn't anyone see him?"

"I saw someone coming out of the inlet," tall, dark-haired Allen Bates contributed. "I guess he could be the one who ran into you, but where did he go?"

For a moment, they all looked at each other in silence. Then the stillness was torn by the snarl of a motor.

"Probably to ride his yellow snowmobile," Linda said, her eyes on Randy Fox.

"Well, how about some hot chocolate and chili?" Randy asked, his face glowing a deeper red as he avoided her gaze. "That's what Mrs White has waiting for us. Unless you want to skate some more?" He looked at Linda, his gaze a challenge.

"Actually, I think I've had about enough for one day," Linda replied, smiling at the rest of the Saddle Club members, while not looking at Randy. "Besides, we can't get acquainted out here."

Bob took her arm and they began skating back around the outcropping towards the bonfire. The others followed as Linda leaned gratefully on her brother, her knees still weak from the shock of the sudden attack.

"Do you know who attacked you?" Bob asked as they neared the bonfire.

Linda shook her head. "I couldn't see anything but his eyes, and he didn't say anything." She grinned at him. "I didn't see a yellow snowmobile, either."

"Randy looked as though he did," Bob replied. "You okay?"

"I should be getting used to being knocked down," Linda quipped. "First those men last night, now this."

"Do you think the attacks are related?" Bob asked.

"I think he was after the stone this time. If the chain hadn't gotten tangled in my scarf, he probably would have been able to break it and get the stone. Thank goodness you came so fast."

"I was looking for you before I heard you scream," Bob admitted.

"I guess I shouldn't have skated so far away from everybody."

Bob started to comment, then said nothing as Mrs White came out of the house and down the stone stairs to the shore. "Are you all ready for something hot to eat?" she asked.

"That sounds wonderful," Linda answered, giving Bob a warning glance and hoping that he wouldn't mention the attack at that moment.

"Randy said something about chili," Bob said.

"I hope you like it," Mrs White told him, then began calling to the others to shed their skates and come into the recreation room for food.

Though the company was pleasant and the hot food a perfect antidote to the cold and fright she'd felt, Linda was relieved when the members of the Saddle Club said good-bye and trooped out into the snowy night, leaving them alone with the Whites and their grandparents. Linda took a deep breath, not sure exactly where to begin her story.

Bob saved her the trouble by immediately telling them about the mysterious skater in the green and black ski mask. Doña came over at once. "Are you all right, Linda?" she asked, her dark eyes full of concern.

"I'm fine," Linda assured her. "Just confused."

"What do you mean?" Bronco asked.

"Well, last night the men were after the sleigh, but today the man who knocked me down was after this." She held the black stone in her hand. "What in the world would anyone want with it?"

After a moment, they all turned to look at Mrs White. She shook her head. "I'm afraid I have no idea," she told them. "Unless there is something about it in the journal you found."

"Why don't we read it and find out?" Mr White suggested.

"I could read it aloud to you," Mrs White agreed. "I mean, if you don't think you'd be bored to death."

"I'd love to hear it," Linda said. "I'm sure there must be something about this stone and about the sleigh, but . . ." She stopped, her gaze suddenly shifting to the far wall. "What's that?" she asked, getting to her feet and crossing to look for herself.

"Oh, that's right, you didn't hear our news." Mrs White followed her, switching on a lamp that illuminated the large, elegant carving. "That's 'The Old Sleigh'. It was returned to us last night."

"Returned?" Bob joined them.

Mrs White sighed. "I don't understand it either," she admitted, "but I'm too happy to ask any questions. I went out to dinner with friends last night since John was away, and when I came home, it was just there—as if it had never been away."

"You mean, whoever took it just brought it back?" Linda asked, having found her voice.

"That seems to be what happened," Bronco confirmed.

"But if they wanted it bad enough to steal it . . ." Linda began, then stopped, realizing that no one else would know the answer to her question either. "Curiouser and curiouser," she finished lamely.

"First someone takes the carving of the sleigh," Bob said, "then they try to steal the sleigh itself. Then they return the picture and try to steal the stone that was hidden in the sleigh." He shook his head. "None of it makes the slightest bit of sense."

"Maybe the journal will explain it," Doña suggested.

"What about Melanie Davis?" Linda asked, returning to her cushion on the floor near the fireplace. "What do you know about her, Mrs White? I mean, you said something about her being a part of a mystery."

Mrs White sank down in a padded rocker near the fire. "Melanie Davis is a mystery," she began. "She and her sister, my mother Anne, grew up on this ranch. It belonged to my grandfather, the same man who carved the sleigh and the picture, plus a number of other things. Anyway, Melanie and Anne were the only children, and when Grandpa and Grandma died in an influenza epidemic, the girls inherited the ranch. However, by that time, Melanie had disappeared. Mum was already married to my father, so they stayed here and ran the ranch."

"Very well," Mr White contributed. "It was only about ten years ago that things got too hard for them and they sold some of the land to developers. They never stopped looking for Melanie, though. When

46

we took over the place, I found reports from five different private investigators that they had received at different times."

"Private investigators?" Linda was surprised.

"Trying to locate Melanie," Mrs White supplied. "But they never found a trace. That's why I'm so excited about this book. This just might tell us what really happened to Melanie."

"What do you mean—really happened?" Linda asked. "What did they think happened?"

Mrs White sighed. "My mother never believed it, but she told me that there was a lot of talk at the time Melanie disappeared. Something about some treasure that she was supposed to have taken with her."

"A treasure?" Bob sat forward. "What was it?"

"Mum didn't know. My grandfather was a very stern old man, I guess. Melanie and Mum were born late in his life and he wasn't very close to them. I never knew him at all, since he died before I was born. Mum didn't talk about him very much, but she did tell me once that Melanie was his favourite and that after she left, he refused to even speak her name or allow anyone to say it in his presence. All he did say was that she'd taken his treasure, not what it was or why or anything."

"Then there really is a treasure," Linda gasped, her fingers rising to touch the stone, which was warm from her skin.

"There was something," Mrs White agreed, "but we won't know what unless it's in this." She opened the journal and began to read, stumbling a little over the faded handwriting.

Linda leaned back and closed her eyes, listening closely as the journal described the world as it had

47

been so long ago. What she heard was fascinating, but disappointing, too. For there was no mention of a treasure, just the day-by-day account of the life of two teenage girls in Montana seventy years ago.

There were pages of description of the preparations for Anne's wedding to Enos Landsburg and Melanie's joy at her sister's happiness. Then the tone of the journal began to change. Linda sat forward as Mrs White read one particular passage.

Father is growing more resentful of Enos. He's asked me to take the treasure from the house and put it in a new place. He's even trusted me to make the black keys to mark the spot. He's sworn me to secrecy, so I can't even tell Anne what is going on. That makes me sad, since I'm sure that Father is wrong to distrust Enos.

The next entries were more routine and there were few pages that even mentioned the mysterious treasure again. Linda shook her head, trying to force the cobwebs from her sleepy mind so she could concentrate better.

I'm afraid that Father is trying to make trouble between Anne and me. If it weren't for Calvin, I don't believe I could bear to stay on in the same house with the rest of them. I wish I dared tell Anne about the treasure, but I know she keeps nothing from Enos, and if Father found out . . .

Perhaps Anne will find this journal in the sleigh, then she'll understand. We were together when Father showed us the secrets of the carvings, so she could find it if she chose to look. I must try again to convince Father that he can trust Anne. I can't bear feeling so separated from her.

Mrs White sighed and closed the book over her finger. "Mother mentioned that time," she said softly, her voice faintly hoarse from so much reading. "She never knew why Melanie grew so distant, though she did know that Grandfather distrusted everyone, including my father."

"What about your grandmother?" Doña asked. "Couldn't she make peace between them?"

Mrs White shook her head. "It was a troubled household, Roz," she admitted. "I don't know the whole story, but I suspect that my grandfather was failing mentally long before his death and he evidently became suspicious of everyone, even my grandmother. Then, too, she'd suffered some kind of fall and was partially bedridden, which was why my parents stayed on in this house after they married instead of moving to a home of their own. Caring for the ranch and both parents was far too much for Melanie to manage alone."

"She certainly doesn't tell us much about the treasure," Linda murmured, "not even what it is."

"I wish I could tell you more," Mrs White said, "but Mother never talked much about her childhood. I guess a lot of her memories were sad. She always said that the sleigh and the carving of it were her treasures, but till now, I didn't realize that there might be another very valuable treasure."

"Does Melanie say anything else?" Linda asked.

"The last page is blank," Mrs White answered, then sighed and handed her the book. "Why don't you look through this some more tomorrow?" she suggested. "Maybe there's a clue that we've missed because we're all tired and sleepy."

Linda got to her feet. "I'd better take Rango out for a few minutes," she said, "and check on Chica and Rocket."

"I'll go with you," Bob said, calling the contentedly sleeping dog away from the fire.

"So what do you think, Sis?" he asked once they were out in the still cold of the night.

Linda shrugged. "It makes more sense if the thief is after this mysterious treasure," she said. "But how could anyone else know about it? And how would they know that the journal was in the sleigh? I found it purely by accident."

The snow crunched loudly under their feet as they crossed to the stable. "Do you think there could be more clues in the sleigh?" Bob asked, peering towards the corner of the stable where the beautiful old vehicle now rested.

"I wish I knew. Do you think it's safe here?"

Bob frowned. "I'll go and ask Mr White about locking up. You keep an eye on Rango—make sure he doesn't chase a rabbit into the woods and get lost."

Linda nodded, stepping back outside to watch as the big dog bounded through the snow. Then, suddenly, he stopped, his big body stiffening as he sniffed the air.

"What is it, boy?" Linda asked, slipping and sliding through the snow to his side.

A low, rumbling growl was his only answer, and he moved forward carefully, stalking into the deep shadows beneath the pines that protected one side of the big log building. Linda followed him cautiously, feeling safer because she could see Bronco and Doña and Mrs White through the nearby window. The light from it spilled out, and as Rango paused, she noticed that the snow beneath the window was well marked with footprints.

Were those footprints there earlier? Linda wondered. So many people had been around the house; some of them could have passed this way, but . . .

Rango plunged forward, snarling and barking, and disappeared into the trees. Linda raced after him, remembering Bob's warning not to let the dog get lost in the unfamiliar territory of the snowy mountains. "Rango," she shouted. "Rango, come back here!"

It was difficult running, for the snow was rough under the pines and Linda couldn't see where she was going in the dark. Suddenly, her foot was snared by something solid under the snow and she went down. "Rango!" she cried again, before her face was buried in the snow.

There was a mocking roar of a snowmobile motor in the distance, and as she scrambled to her feet again, she could hear shouts coming from the house. A warm, wet nose pushed into her cold hand, and Rango whined in concern. She was so glad to see him, she hugged him before trudging back to explain what had happened to Bob and Mr White.

"Are you sure there was someone there?" Mr White asked when she finished. "I mean, did you see anyone?"

Linda shook her head. "But Rango did. And I heard a snowmobile starting right after I fell."

Mr White smiled. "That's not exactly a rare sound around here, Linda," he reminded her. "And there are cabins close by. You can't see them through the trees. However, we will padlock the stable door and make sure the house is locked tonight."

Linda nodded, not really reassured. She was convinced that someone had been watching and listening to what Mrs White was reading from the old journal. She carried that worry to bed with her, along with the precious journal, and her sleep was light because of it.

Morning proved her fear wrong. The sleigh was still in the stable, and the journal rested where she'd left it on her nightstand.

"Want to try skating again?" Bob asked after they finished breakfast.

"Yes," Linda answered, "I . . ." She stopped as the doorbell rang.

"Will you get that?" Mrs White called.

Linda opened the door to find some of yesterday's new friends on the other side. She invited them in.

Allen Bates shook his head. "No use tracking snow in. We were just wondering if you and Bob would like to go tobogganing with us."

"It's a long, hard hike to the run," Diane warned her, "but it's terrific fun."

Linda looked up at Bob, who'd joined her. "What do you think?" she asked.

"Sounds good to me," he said. "Where is the run?"

"Right over there." Allen pointed to a break in the forested flank of the mountain that rose from the lake. "There was a snowslide there a couple of years ago. It took all the timber out, so in the winter it makes a great run."

"How do you get there?" Bob inquired.

"There's a trail," Randy answered. "It takes forever to drag the toboggan up, but the ride is spectacular."

"Could a horse make it up the trail?" Linda inquired.

"To the top of the run?" Allen asked. "Sure. We ride that way sometimes in the summer."

"How would it be if we let our horses tow the toboggan to the top?" Bob asked.

"The trail is too narrow and twisting for a team," Randy answered emphatically.

Linda eyed Chica. "How about one horse?"

"We don't have a harness," Allen warned.

"We could rig something," Bob offered hopefully.

Diane smiled. "It sounds wonderful to me. I'm always so tired after the hike up there, I can never make more than a couple of runs. Hauling the toboggan back up the run is hard."

"Let's ask the Whites," Linda suggested, "and Bronco and Doña."

Permission was quickly given, and Mr White came to the stable to help fix a harness for Chica to wear for the trek to the top of the hill. "Just be sure to take her blanket along," he counselled, "and don't let her just stand in the snow too long. She'll need to move around to keep warm."

"Don't worry if we're not here when you get back," Mrs White called from the kitchen as Linda came in to say goodbye. "We have some errands to do in town and we'll probably all go in together."

"See you later, then." Linda hurried out to join the others who were already seated on the toboggan.

"Think you can ride her with the harness?" Randy asked, smirking nastily. "She looks wild."

Linda gave him a disgusted glare, then vaulted onto the filly's back, carefully placing her legs just ahead of the ropes that led back to the toboggan. Chica bounced forward, then stopped in surprise when the toboggan dragged along behind her.

"It's all right, girl," Linda assured her, stroking the arched neck. "We're just going to take a few friends for a ride."

Chica responded by moving forward sedately till the ropes tightened and the toboggan began to slide over the rutted snow. Shouts and cheers rose from the passengers, and Rango barked joyously as he bounded alongside.

"The trail to the top of the run starts just beyond that bent pine," Allen called, and Linda guided the willing filly in that direction.

The trail was narrow and quite rough. Linda was proud of the way Chica scrambled through the often deep snow, dragging the toboggan easily. "How much farther is it?" Linda asked after a while as she sensed that her palomino was just beginning to tire.

"Around the next bend," Allen answered.

"Is Chica getting tired, Sis?" Bob asked.

"She's not used to the snow," Linda replied.

"My horse would have dropped by now," Diane stated.

"It really is a long way," Bob said. "Isn't there any other way to the run?"

"'Fraid not," Allen answered. "This trail is the closest."

Linda gasped as they moved suddenly from the shadowy trail to the almost blinding glare on the open crest of a ridge. Sunshine sparkled on the sweep of snow that blanketed the toboggan run, but there was also a lot of fairly open area along the top of the ridge where the wind had swept the snow away and left rock and dry grass. She stopped the tired filly and slid off her back.

"Let me help you," Allen offered, coming to unfasten the harness, then using a burlap bag to rub Chica down before he and Linda buckled the red blanket over her golden body.

"I think I can just turn her loose up here," Linda said. "She won't wander far, and she can graze a little."

"I'm for trying the run," Bob told her as she led Chica away from the others, who were busy positioning the toboggan on the top of the slope.

"I'd better wait with Chica the first time," Linda said. "She might be afraid alone."

"I'll stay with her," Diane volunteered, petting the filly. "I've been down the run a dozen times already this winter."

Linda took little persuading before she found herself sandwiched between Allen and Bob on the toboggan. "Hang on tight," Allen warned. "Once we get started, there's no way to stop it till we reach the bottom, and the only steering is by leaning. Just do what I do, and . . ."

The rest of his words were lost as Randy, who was the last passenger on the toboggan, gave a gigantic push, then leaped into his spot as the heavy sled began gathering speed. Linda lost her breath as the icy air whipped by, and the up-curved front of the toboggan bounced over the ridges and gullies the wind had made in the snow.

It was wildly exciting—a little like riding a roller coaster and a lot like being astride a runaway horse. The wind brought tears to Linda's eyes and froze them on her cheeks. Allen leaned to the right, steering the speeding toboggan around an ugly-looking stump, then leaned back to the left, easing their headlong flight onto a broad stretch of ice-crusted snow that let them fly even faster.

Linda gasped, suddenly aware that the lake was rushing at them in terrifying fashion. Were they going to crash on the shore? What in the world would stop them? There was no time to ask. Allen leaned left once again, and the flying toboggan eased off the straight chute to the lake and began to slow as it hit a slight upgrade and softer snow.

Then it was over. The silence was as deafening as the roar of the wind had been. Linda felt strangely stiff as she got to her feet. She looked back up the side of the mountain, shocked to see how small Chica and Diane looked.

"Did you like it?" Allen asked.

"It was wonderful," she murmured, hardly recognizing her own voice. "Only, how do you ever keep from hitting something or ending up on the lake?"

"Practice," Randy answered. "And hitting the lake isn't too bad. You can skid halfway across before you stop. It's the walk back that's bad."

"We go home that way," Allen explained. "The lake is frozen all the way across at this end, so it's an easy walk to my house after we stop."

"Now comes the tough part," Randy said. "We have to climb back up."

Linda groaned. "You need a toboggan lift," she teased. "Like a ski lift. We could be hauled up and fly back down."

Everyone agreed and, still laughing, they grabbed the ropes and began the slow, hard climb to the top. The path they used was close to the toboggan run, but much of it was rough and rocky, which made it a tough climb. Linda was tired by the time they reached the top.

"Ready to go again?" Allen asked, once they caught their breath.

"I'll stay with Chica this time," Linda said.

"I don't think you need to worry about her," Diane reassured her. "Look."

Linda looked, then laughed. Chica, obviously bored with the humans' foolishness, had wandered along the ridge and was busily trying to nibble some grass out from between two big rocks.

"She didn't even jump when you took off," Diane continued.

"So why don't we all go?" Randy suggested.

Linda hesitated, watching as Chica moved on with Rango at her side. Then she shrugged. "I guess she won't miss me, and she is moving around, like Mr White said."

The second ride down was less terrifying, though the climb back to the ridge seemed longer. A third ride and a fourth when they nearly hit the stump were enough for Linda. She looked at her watch as they neared the top.

"I wonder if we shouldn't be thinking about the long trek back," she suggested, noting that it was getting close to noon.

"I've been thinking about that, too," Randy said, "and I have an idea."

"What's that?" Bob asked. Randy had been friendly through most of the morning, but Linda sensed that Bob still didn't trust the burly boy.

"Well, Linda and the horse could get back a lot faster if she didn't have to drag the toboggan down that trail, and we could make it fast if we tobogganed across the end of the lake." Randy smiled.

"I don't think Linda should have to ride back all alone," Bob protested, but Linda could see him casting a longing glance at the toboggan. He obviously wanted to try the wild ride on the ice.

"It's not that far," Linda said. "And there isn't any way I can get lost on that trail."

"Without the toboggan to pull, you'll probably beat us down," Allen contributed.

Linda started to answer, then frowned as she realized that Rango was limping. She called him over to examine his paw. "What's the matter, fella?" she asked.

"Looks like an ice cut," Allen observed as he bent his dark head close to hers. "My collie gets them every winter."

"He can't walk home on that," Linda said. "It's much too far."

"Why don't we take him on the toboggan?" Bob suggested.

"It's all right with me," Allen said, looking at the others. Everyone nodded but Randy.

"What if he gets scared and tips us over?" Randy asked. "He could make a lot of trouble."

"Oh, come on, we took Shep with us last time and he loved it," Allen replied. "Bob can ride behind me, and we'll put the dog between us."

Randy looked as though he'd like to argue, then shrugged, obviously remembering that the toboggan belonged to Allen. Linda felt him watching her while she checked Chica's hooves for ice balls, which Mr White had cautioned her about. She decided to leave the horse blanket on her for the ride down to the house.

"Want me to give you a leg up?" Randy asked as the rest of the group moved to the toboggan. "You don't want to pull the blanket out of place getting on."

"Thank you," Linda said, surprised by the offer and realizing his warning was correct.

"Before you start down, you ought to ride over near the cliff and take a good look out over the

They were racing an avalanche!

lake," Randy advised, lifting her onto the filly's back. "It's a great view of the whole area."

"I will, and thanks for telling me, Randy. You all have a nice ride down."

"We will," Randy called over his shoulder as he ran to push the toboggan and leap aboard as it started down the mountain once again.

Linda sighed and reined Chica away from the toboggan run, heading towards the rising cliff of the mountain. The ground directly below the cliff had been scoured free of snow by the wind, but the cliff itself was heavy with the drifted winter's accumulation. Linda looked up at it rather dubiously as they approached, then she looked ahead.

The spot that Randy had indicated was right under the cliff, where the ridge dropped abruptly towards the lake and the valley around it. Chica began to dance and shy away from the path that Linda had been following. Linda stopped her at once.

"What is it, Chica?" she asked.

The filly stood still for a moment. Then Linda heard the distant rumbling. Not sure what it meant, she wrapped her fingers in the filly's heavy white mane and clenched her knees as tightly as she could.

Chica squealed and reared, then spun around and began racing, slipping and sliding, back the way they'd come. The thunder grew louder, but Linda only bent closer to the filly's neck, praying that her horse's small hooves wouldn't slip or falter. She knew now that they were racing an avalanche!

Cold snow pursued Linda and Chica as the filly plunged into the shadowy confines of the trail. She raced wildly around the first two curves, then slowed, and finally stopped, her whole body shivering. For a moment, Linda just lay against her neck, shaking as hard as the horse. Then she drew in a shuddering breath and lifted her head.

The rumbling had stopped and the world around them looked much as it had on the way to the toboggan run. Linda forced her stiff fingers to release Chica's mane, and she stroked the filly's wet neck.

"Are you all right, Chica?" she asked as the palomino turned her lovely head around to sniff at her knee. "You didn't hurt yourself?"

Chica gave herself a shake that nearly unseated Linda, then began moving forward calmly, her stride steady as she followed the winding trail that still bore the marks of the toboggan. Linda tried to look back, but the thick-growing fir trees hid the ridge from her.

Linda straightened up, taking several deep breaths to quiet her pounding heart. She tried not to think about the cascading snow and how close it had come to sweeping her and Chica over the cliff.

Suddenly, she thought of Bob and their new friends. Were they safe? But the toboggan went so quickly she was sure they'd been out on the lake before she rode to the cliff.

"Did you know it was coming, Chica?" she asked

the filly, remembering how she'd refused to go closer to the cliff edge. "You saved our lives by not going over there."

Chica snorted, then began to trot through the shadowy stillness, obviously anxious to return to the safety of the warm stable. Linda didn't try to slow her, since she, too, had had enough of the mountain for one day.

The house and stable were quiet and empty when they reached them. Rocket whinnied a greeting to Chica, and Linda checked the filly over carefully before putting her in her stall. Miraculously, the palomino seemed to have come through her wild flight without a scratch. Linda was just closing her stall when Bob entered the stable carrying the harness.

"Allen was right," he greeted her. "He said you'd beat us down."

"I almost beat you to the lake," Linda told him, then described what had happened.

"An avalanche?" Bob gasped. "Gosh, we didn't see anything like that from the lake. Are you sure?"

"It sounded like a freight train," Linda said, "and if Chica hadn't heard it and run for the trail, I'm sure we would have been carried down the mountain."

"What were you doing over there, anyway?" Bob inquired.

"I was going to look at the view," Linda answered. "Randy said you could see the whole valley."

"Well, I'm glad Chica was so smart," Bob told her, reaching over to give the filly a pat, "but right now I'm starving. Walking on the lake is a lot easier than in the snow, but it was still a long way."

"Where's Rango?" Linda asked, missing the dog.

"I put him on the service porch to dry off before we put salve on his paw."

"Is anybody home?" Linda inquired.

Bob shook his head. "According to the note, lunch is in the oven, and believe me, it smells super." He put his arm around her shoulders. "You sure you're all right?"

Linda nodded, feeling better. "I guess I was just a little shaken up. It all happened so fast, and I felt so all alone there."

"Next time, I'll ride Rocket up so we can come back together," Bob promised.

"If there is a next time," Linda said, her taste for tobogganing considerably dampened.

"The whole gang is coming over to skate this afternoon," Bob informed her as they walked across the yard to the house. "They say the smoothest ice is at this end of the lake."

"They really seem to be nice," Linda remarked as she sniffed the scents coming from the kitchen and realized that she was starving. "At least, most of them are."

Bob chuckled. "I think Randy is just trying to impress you, Sis."

"Well, he's not making a very good impression," Linda snapped. Then she added, "Why don't you fix Rango's paw while I get our lunch ready?" She was aware that Bob was amused at her attitude, and it irritated her.

"Allen says it will heal without anything," Bob told her. "Rango just has to stay out of icy snow for a couple of days. It's really a tiny cut, but the ice gets in the fur between his paw pads and stabs into it. That's why he was limping."

Linda was sceptical of the explanation, but when Bob opened the door to the service porch, the big dog had scarcely a trace of his earlier limp. Linda grinned at him. "I'll bet he just wanted a ride on the toboggan," she teased.

"He loved it," Bob confirmed, "but he limped all the way home on the lake. I'll apply some salve on the pad, just in case."

Linda nodded, already busy putting lunch on the table. She sighed happily when they both sat down. "Bronco and Doña don't know what they're missing," she observed after her first bite.

"They seem to be having a good time," Bob said. "I get the feeling that they used to spend a lot of time with the Whites before they moved away."

Linda nodded, her mind returning to the main reason for their visit to Montana. "What do you think about the journal?" she asked.

"It's interesting, but Melanie certainly didn't bother to put in many details," Bob answered. "Or did I miss a clue in last night's reading?"

"Well, I have been thinking about one thing," Linda began.

"What's that?"

"The black keys."

"What about them?" Bob looked mystified.

"Well, why would anyone paint a key black?" Linda didn't wait for an answer, since she was pretty sure that Bob didn't have one. "And why have more than one key, if the treasure was locked away somewhere?"

Bob drank some of his milk, his lightly freckled face thoughtful. "You're right," he said. "But what do you think it means?"

Linda sighed. "I'm not sure, but I was wondering if Melanie could mean keys as ways of solving something. Like the key to a code."

Bob considered it. "And what if she does?"

"Then this could be one of the black keys." Linda fumbled at the neck of her sweater and lifted the chain and black stone out.

Bob nodded. "That could explain your mysterious attacker yesterday."

"Not really," Linda protested. "How would he know about the stone and what it means—if it means anything at all?"

"Well, if the man on the yellow snowmobile is involved, he could have seen the stone when you tried to give it to Mrs White. That is, if he was really watching us and if he had binoculars."

"But I couldn't see him because of the plane, so he couldn't see me either," Linda reminded him.

"He could have moved to another area to look."

"That's pretty thin evidence," Linda murmured.

"Also, it doesn't explain the disappearance and return of the wall carving," Bob said. "Or the attempt to steal the sleigh."

Linda shook her head. "Nothing makes sense."

"So let's finish lunch and go skating," Bob suggested. "And tomorrow we're invited on a trail ride with the Saddle Club. Allen says they can't go too far because of the snow, but they try to get out as often as they can in the winter just to keep their horses in condition."

"When did he tell you about the ride?" Linda asked.

"While we were walking back." Bob paused "You want to go, don't you?"

"Of course," Linda replied, turning her attention to her food.

As they were gathering up the dishes, Rango barked and ran to the door, his tail wagging. "That must be the family coming home," Bob said.

"Let's not mention the avalanche," Linda suggested.

"Why not?" Bob asked, surprised.

"Well, we don't want to worry them tomorrow, and since you said you didn't see or hear anything . . ." Her voice trailed off.

"I was probably halfway across the lake when it happened," Bob reminded her.

"Even so . . ."

Bob nodded. "I guess they might decide not to let us ride tomorrow."

"Maybe it was just a little snowslide and I got excited because Chica was scared." Linda knew even as she spoke that she was trying to reassure herself. It had been very real on the mountain.

"I think we should tell Allen," Bob said. "He's the president of the junior saddle club, and he should know if that area is going to be dangerous."

Linda nodded, then went to open the door for the four laughing adults. Their cheerful tales quickly banished the last of the shadows over Linda's mind, and she joined in with stories of her own. They were all still in the kitchen talking when the first of the skaters arrived.

The afternoon flew by as the young people explored the lake and frozen inlet, then danced on the ice to music from a transistor radio. Late in the afternoon, when Linda was skating with Allen, she mentioned the avalanche as casually as she could.

"I'm sorry you were frightened by a snowslide,"

Allen told her. "They can be scary, and dangerous, too. That cliff area has been unstable since the big slide that made our toboggan run. We stay away from it in the winter."

"Luckily, Chica heard it start," Linda said, wondering if she should tell him that Randy had suggested she ride along the cliff.

"Well, we'll steer clear of that area tomorrow," Allen promised. "There are lots of other nice places to ride, even in the winter, and as long as the good weather holds, we want to enjoy it as much as possible."

"Allen, what causes a snowslide?" Linda asked.

"Snow melting, mostly," Allen answered. "It will get soft underneath, or it gets slushy on top, and once it starts to move—" He shrugged. "Or sometimes water seeps into a crack in the rock and freezes. That means it expands, and if it expands enough, it can crack the rock and cause it to slide. That will bring the snow down, too."

Linda nodded. "Well, I'm glad it didn't wipe out the toboggan run," she said.

"That was fun, wasn't it?" Allen began whirling her, then spinning himself till they were both so dizzy they could only drop on the old log near the bonfire that Mr White had lit.

"I'm going to have to go home pretty soon," he said, "I've got chores."

Linda smiled. "I have to go up and feed Chica, too. Besides, I want to check her legs and make sure she didn't strain any muscles or tendons running away from the slide."

"Just so she isn't lame tomorrow," Allen said.

He left to skate across the lake to his home, which was just visible through the trees now that lights were burning in the windows. Tired, Linda unfastened her skates. She was slipping her feet into her boots when she heard a whinny coming from the stable. It was followed by a crash.

"Chica!" Linda gasped, leaving her skates and running up the slippery steps. As she ran past the house, she could hear a squeal of anger from the stable. The door was standing open and as she ran inside, she saw that the sleigh was no longer in its corner!

Linda stopped, searching the dark corners of the stable for an intruder. Chica snorted and struck at her stall door again. Linda opened it, taking hold of the filly's halter.

"What's the matter, girl?" she asked, aware that the palomino was trembling with excitement.

Nothing moved in the stable. As her eyes adjusted, she realized that the sleigh was now at the far end of the building near the double doors.

"What's going on here?" Bronco demanded as he rushed in. "Is something wrong with Chica? I saw you run by the window."

Linda relaxed a little, glad to have her grandfather beside her. "I think someone was in here," she said. "The door was open and the sleigh has been moved."

Bronco switched on the lights and moved across the stable to examine the sleigh and the runner marks that showed that it had been dragged from its corner. He was frowning when he looked up at her. "There's no way to find footprints under all the straw," he said, "but the runner marks are clear. What made you come up here?"

"Chica raised a fuss," Linda answered.

"I'll go tell John," Bronco said. "It looks like whoever was here must have run when Chica raised an alarm. Probably realized we'd come to check on her."

Linda nodded, her arm around the filly's neck. She had returned Chica to her stall by the time the men came to put the sleigh back in place. Linda and Bob fed the horses while Mr White checked the stable doors and windows, locking up after they finished.

"I don't like it," Mr White said as they walked back. "I've never had to lock things up."

"I wish I knew what they want with the sleigh," Linda murmured.

"Maybe there's something we missed in the journal," Bob suggested.

"I'll get it," Linda said, heading for the bedroom she'd been using. "Maybe if we read every word . . ."

Her room was untidy, her clothes from the toboggan ride still drying on the back of the chair while her half-unpacked suitcase sat on the cedar chest in the corner. Linda sighed and reached under the pillow for the journal. Her fingers touched cool sheets, nothing else.

Frowning, she tried the other side. Nothing! Feeling sick, she turned back the bedspread and lifted both pillows. The sheets were white and fresh, but Melanie's journal was gone!

Already sure of the outcome, Linda began a methodical search of the room, peering into, under, and behind everything. After twenty frantic minutes, she was no closer to finding the journal than she had been in the beginning.

"Linda?" Bob stood in the doorway. "What's going on?" he asked.

"The journal isn't here," Linda answered. "It's disappeared."

"What?"

Linda explained that she'd hidden it under her pillow when she made her bed that morning, finishing, "I've just looked everywhere, so unless someone in the house has it . . ."

His expression told her he didn't think that was the case. "What'll we do?" he asked.

"I guess we'd better tell them," Linda said, wishing she could just disappear herself.

The Whites were shocked and saddened by the news, but showed no sign of blaming Linda for the loss. "I guess it would have been easy for anyone to get in," Mr White admitted. "We never think to lock the house when we leave during the day."

"That shows that someone was watching last night when you read the journal, Beatrice," Doña observed. "Someone who decided it would help him find the treasure."

"You really think that old treasure tale is behind all this?" Mrs White asked.

"What else could it be?" Bronco said. "The question is—how could they know about it before Linda found the journal?"

"Before?" Mr White looked sceptical.

"The carving," Linda gasped, following Bronco's line of thought. "That was stolen even before we knew the sleigh was in the shed."

"And it was returned as soon as the thief found out that the real sleigh existed," Bronco agreed.

"Who would know about the sleigh so quickly?" Bob asked. "There were only a couple of days from our call till the parade."

Mrs White sighed. "I'm afraid anyone in the area could have known about your finding the sleigh. I was so excited, I told everybody."

"What about the treasure?" Linda inquired. "Who would have known about that?"

That answer came less quickly as the Whites exchanged glances. "It was common gossip when the journal was written," Mr White murmured, "and I think there was something in the local paper when Beatrice inherited this place. But that was close to ten years ago."

"Nothing more recent?" Linda asked.

"Not that I've heard," Mrs White replied. "It's just a part of the history of the area, nothing more."

"Someone doesn't seem to believe that," Bronco reminded them, and Linda felt a chill at his words. She remembered the rough men in the shed and the force of the man in the ski mask when he'd tried to steal the stone. Whoever was after the treasure was obviously in deadly earnest, and they had no way of knowing who it might be.

"So what do we do next?" Bob asked.

"I would suggest dinner," Mrs White replied, getting to her feet. "You must be starving after all that skating."

The evening was pleasant, but Linda was glad when she could slip off to bed. Her thoughts were not good companions, and her sleep was restless.

Linda woke to a beautiful clear morning, a perfect day for the Saddle Club ride. She pulled on her clothes quickly, hating the need for coats every time she stepped outside the door.

She picked up the stable key and let herself and Rango out in the early morning light. The loss of the journal had made her worry about the sleigh, and she was relieved to find it safely in the stable.

Once she'd finished the morning chores, Linda turned her attention to the sleigh. Having learned more about the man who did the carving, and the people who'd used the vehicle, made it seem even more precious. She caressed the perfectly executed wing feathers with gentle fingers.

The man must have spent months, perhaps years working on it, she realized. Had they used it often after it was finished? It was hard to picture anyone casually choosing to ride in such an elegant work of art.

She climbed into the sleigh and opened the secret compartment, wishing now that the journal had been hidden there instead of in her bed.

"Looking for something?" Bob asked, startling her so that she nearly fell out of the sleigh.

"I was just wishing that I'd put the journal out here yesterday," Linda admitted.

"If our thief had taken the sleigh, you would have lost it anyway," Bob reminded her.

"I just feel bad about it."

"Do you think there could be other secret compartments in this sleigh?" Bob asked.

Linda shrugged, tracing the delicate carving of the swan's neck. "I suppose," she answered, "there could be a half-dozen of them, the way this is done."

"Do you think the treasure is hidden in it?"

A quick denial came to her lips, but she hesitated a moment before answering. "It depends on what the stone means," she finally said. "If this stone is one of the black keys Melanie wrote about, then I doubt that she'd hide the treasure in the same place where she put the keys. Besides, even a sleigh like this would be something you'd use, and it would be pretty easy to steal."

Bob chuckled. "Not too easy," he reminded her, opening the stable door to admit Rango, "thanks to Rango and Chica."

Linda laughed. "So what's going on in the house?"

"Mrs White was starting breakfast and Doña was talking about preparing a picnic for us to take with us on the ride."

"A picnic in the snow?" Linda didn't hide her scepticism.

"That's what I said," Bob admitted, "but Mrs White says the ride will take us to someplace called Crestline. It's not exactly a house, but there's shelter there and facilities for building a fire and tables and everything."

"It sounds a little strange, but I guess I'm game to try it," Linda said, smiling. "It can't be any worse than that first toboggan ride."

"That was pretty wild," Bob agreed, "but it sure was fun, too."

Linda nodded, wishing that she didn't keep remembering the rumbling threat of the snowslide that had followed it. She shivered, though the stable wasn't cold.

"So let's go and have breakfast," Bob suggested. "We've got plenty to do before the ride."

In spite of her doubts, Linda loved the chill air and the clear blue sky that stretched above the snow-wrapped peaks. They'd been joined by about twenty more riders, which made remembering names impossible. Still, everyone was friendly and she soon found herself riding with Allen and Diane as well as Bob.

The ride was beautiful. Once they left the shelter of the thick forest, the vistas of sky, mountains, and lake below were breathtaking. Still, Linda forced herself to keep a part of her attention on the trail, for she worried about Chica's inexperience with snow and ice.

She'd been concentrating on the rocky ledge they were following when Allen suddenly reined in and gasped. "Would you look at that?" he demanded of no one in particular.

Linda looked up and caught her breath sharply. The mountain ahead of them sparkled in the sunshine, but it clearly was not a normal cliff face. Rocks were gouged from parts of it, and several large trees lay lifeless, their roots drying in the sun.

"There's been a slide in the area," someone observed. "Recently, too."

"This must be where it started," Allen said.

"What do you mean?" Linda asked.

Allen didn't answer, but merely reined his horse to one side and pointed down below.

Linda allowed Chica to move up beside him and looked down at the ridge and small cup of a valley where they'd been yesterday—the top of the toboggan run. Memory of her terror froze any comment in her throat, for much of the little valley was buried under the avalanche that had terrified Chica.

"Good thing we all got out of there when we did," Randy observed, his tone flat and strangely angry. "I had no idea the snow on that cliff face was so unstable."

"We're going to have to be careful if we want to continue to use the toboggan run," Allen agreed, reining his horse back onto the trail. "So let's keep moving. Crestline is just ahead."

Chica followed the other horses, and after a moment, Linda revived enough to answer the questions that Allen was asking about Chica's training. "She's just a very intelligent horse," she told him. "She likes doing things. You can teach her tricks or any sort of riding."

"You mean she does tricks?" Diane asked.

Linda nodded.

"Hey, maybe you could show us a few after lunch," Allen suggested. "What do you say?"

Linda nodded, embarrassed by the attention, but pleased to have people admiring her horse. She was, however, glad when the group moved down from the rocky trail into a sheltered valley where several structures waited.

"Crestline," Allen explained.

The lunch break was fun. Allen and Linda quickly lit fires in two of the firepits and heated the soup and chili that everyone had brought. There was fresh water for the horses, and plenty of food, which the riders shared as they sat around on benches in the slowly warming, half-walled log structure.

"We have dances up here in the summer," Diane said. "It's nicer then, but at least we have some shelter for winter days. I wish you could come back in the summer."

"So do I," Linda admitted.

Once the food was gone, the group moved outside and Linda put Chica through some of her tricks. She had her count and answer yes or no to questions from the group, guided her through a brief dance, then had her bow to her audience.

"Do we ride back the same way?" Linda asked as she helped Diane clear up the debris of their picnic after the trick show was over.

Diane shook her head. "No, we'll go down the back trail. It's on the side of the mountain away from the lake."

"I'm glad," Linda said, "I'd like to see as much of the area as I can."

"It's different, but pretty," Diane commented as she left to throw the napkins and other papers into the fire before the boys used snow to smother it.

The ride down was pleasant. Linda was half dreaming as they followed the trail along the flank of the mountain just above the tree line. She'd forgotten her earlier caution about Chica's footing and was just enjoying the view as they rounded an outcropping of rock.

Chica stopped for a moment and Linda looked out over the rolling folds of the land. There were acres of green-black trees shadowing the snow, but there were also large open areas that looked as though they might be meadows or fields in the summer.

Linda smiled at the tranquil scene, thinking that it

must look now almost the way it had when Melanie and Anne had lived and ridden in this area. Thinking of Melanie reminded her of the missing journal, and she felt a sharp pang of loss as she lifted her gaze from the quiet valley to the mountains that rose above it.

Suddenly she caught her breath, jerking so that Chica took a step forward before Linda tightened the reins to stop her. The mountains were outlined sharply against the clear sky and there was something about the jagged line, the strange bulge of one peak, the uneven cut of another that . . . Fumbling, she unfastened the neck of her parka and pulled the stone free of her clothing so she could see the lines on it.

"What's the matter, Sis?" Bob asked, riding up beside her.

Linda swallowed hard. "I just found out what the stone means," she told him in a whisper.

"What?"

"It's a map, and that area down there is what it marks."

Bob stood in his stirrups to look at the secluded and winter-desolate valley below them. "You mean the treasure is somewhere down there?" he asked without enthusiasm.

Linda could only nod, realizing immediately the hopelessness of her discovery.

"Hey, come on, you two," Allen called from ahead of them. "You won't get home before dark if you keep looking at the scenery."

Linda and Bob exchanged glances, then urged their horses forward. They couldn't explore their discovery now, and without further clues, it looked hopeless. They'd found the meaning of the first black key, but it had only deepened the mystery.

Discovery

The ride back to the Whites' proved easier than Linda had expected, and she carefully marked the trail to the little valley in her mind. Though she longed to spend more time studying the carving on the stone, she restrained herself, conscious that Randy had been watching her ever since those surprising moments on the ridge above the valley.

"Did you enjoy the ride, Linda?" Randy asked, his friendly smile not matching the look in his eyes.

"It was wonderful; this is very pretty country."

"But you didn't come here just to see the sights, did you?" Randy persisted, letting the others ride on while he talked to her.

"What do you mean?" Linda stiffened.

"I thought you were supposed to be smart enough to solve the mystery of who stole Mrs White's sleigh carving." The words were taunting.

"Since the carving was returned, that doesn't seem too important," Linda snapped, wishing that Bob would back out of the stable to see why she and Chica hadn't followed him inside.

"What about the rest of it?" Randy pressed. "Have you found more hidden compartments in the sleigh? And what about the black stone? Do you know what it means?"

"As a matter of fact, the journal has disappeared," Linda stated, changing the subject and watching the obnoxious young man closely. "You wouldn't know anything about that, would you?"

To her surprise, Randy looked totally shocked. "Someone took the journal?" he gasped.

Linda swallowed a sigh, wishing that she hadn't brought it up. "It was . . ." she began, then stopped, relieved to hear a chorus of familiar voices. The Whites, Bronco, and Doña had all come out to welcome them home.

Randy's expression changed, and he called a cheerful goodbye to everyone, then hurried after the other riders. Linda dismounted and led Chica through the narrow doorway into the stable. She quickly told everyone of her discovery.

"Then you think that stone is one of the black keys that Melanie wrote about?" Mrs White asked.

"That would explain why it was hidden with the journal," Linda answered. "And the markings are clear. They show the skyline from that ride, and there is a little x scratched in what has to be that valley."

"Could the treasure be hidden there?" Bronco asked Linda, then turned to the Whites. "What is in that valley?"

"Not much," John answered. "We used to run cattle in the meadows, and it was farmed before that. There's nothing there now, however."

"You own the land?" Bob asked.

Mr White nodded.

"Do you think you can find the treasure, Linda?" Doña asked.

Linda shook her head. "I don't have any idea where to look," she admitted. "The x just marks the valley, nothing more."

"Then there must be more keys," Mrs White said.

They all stared in silence at the handsome old vehicle, and Mrs White finally sighed. "I guess we're not going to figure it out this way," she said, "so we might as well go in and have dinner. Maybe we'll be wiser in the morning."

Linda smiled hopefully, but she didn't think food or sleep would solve the problem. The sleigh had kept its secrets too long, and she doubted that she'd accidentally discover another secret panel.

"I suppose we could have someone take the sleigh apart," Mr White suggested as they ate. "Of course, that might destroy it completely. The wood is old and pretty fragile, but a real craftsman might be able to . . ."

"No." Mrs White's voice was firm. "I won't destroy a real treasure for something that may not even exist. If we can't find the treasure some other way, it will just have to stay hidden."

"I'll do my best," Linda promised, relieved that the sleigh was safe, but feeling the full weight of the responsibility.

"Don't worry about it, dear," Mrs White told her. "You found something very precious when you brought me the journal and the sleigh. The other treasure may just be an old rumour."

"Whoever took the journal doesn't think that," Bob reminded them, and Linda felt a chill.

That thought haunted Linda through the evening and drew her to the sleigh wall carving. It was a lovely work of art, showing Anne and Melanie as little girls on the rear seat of the sleigh, with their parents in the front, their father driving the high-stepping horse.

Trees and distant mountain peaks, a small cabin, and even a bit of lake shore filled in the background with loving detail, but it was the sleigh itself that held her attention. She bent closer.

Every detail of the sleigh had been copied, yet there was something . . .

"Which was done first, Mrs White?" she asked. "The picture or the sleigh?"

Mrs White shrugged. "I have no idea. I don't think anyone ever said. Why? Is it important?"

Linda shook her head. "I guess not. I don't even know why I asked. I suppose that I'm getting desperate. I just feel that it's my fault the journal is gone and I have to do something to make up for it."

Mrs White came over to put her arm around Linda's shoulders. "You mustn't feel that way," she told her sternly. "If it hadn't been for you, I'd never have had the opportunity to read the journal or to know more about my own family. No one can steal that, Linda. And I'll always be grateful."

Linda blinked back a sudden rush of tears. "I guess I'm just tired," she said after she thanked her hostess. "Maybe I do need that good night's sleep."

By morning, her determination had returned. As soon as she could after breakfast, she settled herself in front of the sleigh, trying to find the exact angle of viewing that had been used in the wall carving. Almost at once, she saw what had bothered her last night.

What were lily pads in the actual carving on the sleigh had become an island in the wall hanging. She moved closer, studying the small pads, trying to understand whether this was significant or just an artist's choice to do something different in one work of art than he had in another.

"Find something?" Bob asked, joining her.

Linda explained her observation.

"Maybe the wall carving was done first," Bob suggested, getting a flashlight.

"Or maybe he felt that the lily pads wouldn't show up in the smaller area of the wall carving," Linda agreed. But she was already leaning close, probing at the lily pads, trying to see if one of them concealed a release lever like the one that had been hidden in the footboard.

"See anything?" Bob trained the flashlight on the area.

Linda straightened up with a sigh. "Not a thing. In fact, the pads aren't carved in deep enough to hide anything."

"But it must mean something," Bob mused, moving closer to the sleigh and directing the strong flashlight beam against the intricately marked wood.

Linda moved to one side, then gasped. "There is something," she cried. "Bob, look! Shine the light just that way."

She guided his hand and as she did so, a fine line became obvious. Using her fingernail, she followed it up, turned the sharp corner that was hidden by a tree, then followed it across and down, another corner and along the bottom. "It must be a door," she breathed. "If we could just figure out how to open it."

"Bob, we're about ready to leave," Bronco called from the stable door.

"Blast," Bob grumbled.

"Where are you going?" Linda asked.

"Into town. Didn't you hear the discussion this morning? Mr White is going to take me up in a small plane."

"Oh, sure, I'd forgotten." Linda's attention shifted back to the sleigh.

"What about you?" Bob asked. "Aren't you going shopping with Doña and Mrs White?"

Linda shook her head. "I think I'll stay here."

"You want me to tell everyone you aren't going?" Bob asked.

"Please," Linda replied, then added, "and don't tell them about the line and the lily pads, Bob. I mean, I don't want them to get all excited. It could be that Mr Davis carved the island in that spot first, and then something happened and he redid a part of the panel with the lily pads."

Bob looked as though he'd like to argue, but the others came in to say goodbye to her and to get him so he said nothing. Linda watched them leave with a pang of regret.

Once she turned her attention back to the sleigh, however, all thoughts of town or the airport faded at once. Despite what she'd told Bob, she had no doubt that the line defined another hidden compartment; the problem was to discover how it worked and to see what was inside.

Using the flashlight, she examined every inch of the carving on each side of the seam. There was nothing that she could see. No levers, no buttons, nothing but the smooth, carefully worked wood.

Where in the world can it be? she asked herself, sitting back on her heels. How can I get inside?

The blank eyes of the swan heads looked past her, and the scene shimmered slightly in the uncertain light from the flashlight. Linda glared at it, frustrated and angry enough to have kicked the spot had it been less beautiful.

There has to be a way, she told herself, and the change of design must mean something. One island changed to three lily pads—why? She reached out a hand and touched them meditatively; first the large one, then the two smaller ones.

She heard a *click* and gasped as a square of wood slowly swung open to reveal the compartment behind it. Excitement bubbled up in her throat as she reached inside, her fingers quickly telling her that this compartment contained the same things that the first one had.

The dusty journal was smaller than the other one and the stone was a different shape. But the same handwriting dated the first entry in the journal, and she could feel the familiar ridges of carving on the stone, though the light was too poor for her to make out the marks on it. The panel swung shut again and Linda took a moment to try the hidden releases. It opened.

Well well, she murmured to herself, it looks like I'll have a surprise for everyone when they get home. I just hope . . . She stopped as Rango's bark broke the stillness.

The tone of his bark told her that it wasn't her family returning. Linda hesitated for only a heartbeat, then carried the journal and stone into the darkness of an empty stall, slipping them under the loose hay that lay in the manger. Only then did she head for the door to investigate Rango's alarm.

The sunshine gleamed on the patches of snow that had escaped melting, but there was no sign of a car in the driveway. She couldn't see Rango, but she could hear his excited barking. Linda looked back at her parka, which was hanging on a hook near the tack room, then shrugged, leaving it.

"Rango," she called, "Rango, what is it, boy?"

The barking increased, the tempo changing as though Rango was really after something. Swallowing a sigh, she stepped out the door.

There was a flash of something behind her. Linda started to turn, but before she could take more than a single step, she felt a blow on the side of her head. Everything went black.

Linda stirred, shivering, trying to snuggle under the warm, furry blanket. The blanket moved and a wet tongue caressed her face, forcing her to open her eyes. "Rango," she gasped, realizing that the warm blanket was the dog and that the rest of her body was freezing cold.

Rango whined, licking her again as she tried to sit up. He head throbbed viciously, and the aching cold that seemed to have taken over her body didn't help. "What . . . what happened?" she asked the big dog.

A growl was her answer as Rango stood up, his dark eyes regarding her questioningly, his feathery tail wagging tentatively. Linda touched the back of her head. "Someone must have hit me," she murmured, shivering so violently that for a moment she wasn't sure she could even stand up.

Rango lifted his head; his pricked ears told her that he was listening to something. He barked a cry of welcome and his tail beat the air as the car came up the drive, screeching to a halt. Bob leaped out. "What happened?" he demanded, bending down to help Linda to her feet, then steadying her as she swayed dizzily.

"Someone hit me," Linda murmured, fighting dizziness and nausea. "Rango was barking and I came out to see why and . . . The person must have been beside the door." She stopped, her teeth chattering so hard she could no longer speak.

"Get her in the house," Bronco ordered, stripping off his jacket and putting it around her shoulders. "She's half frozen."

For several minutes there was bedlam as Linda was eased into a kitchen chair and hot tea was brewed for her. Mrs White talked about calling a doctor while the men strode about muttering furiously.

"Rango saved me," Linda said when she recovered. "He came and lay beside me, keeping me warm in the bitter cold. Then he woke me up with his tongue."

"How long were you out there?" Doña asked.

Linda shrugged. "I don't know, I . . ." She stopped as confused memories rushed through her. "The sleigh," she cried. "I found the compartment! There's another notebook and a stone and . . ."

"You what?" Everyone stopped what they were doing and turned to stare at her.

"Come on, I'll show you." Linda got to her feet, the excitement banishing the worst of her weakness and pain.

"Now, I don't think . . ." Doña began, but Linda was already crossing the kitchen and rushing out of the door. She scarcely felt the cold air as she ran across the frozen ground. Terrible fear twisted her stomach even before she looked towards the corner.

"Oh, no," Bob groaned. "It's gone!"

Linda looked from the vacant corner to the stalls and was relieved to see Chica. Feeling sick and shaky, she went over to rest her cheek against the filly's warm neck.

The men searched the stable, following the marks the sleigh had made as it was dragged to the far end. Bob went out and returned with the news that there were truck tracks near the doors.

Bob came over to Linda, his face sad. "I'm sorry, Sis," he said, "but it's really gone this time. They got everything."

Linda looked up at him, more memories filling her mind. "Maybe not," she told him, her depression lifting.

"What do you mean?" Bob asked.

Linda crossed the aisle and slipped into the dark stall. Her fingers dug through the hay. For a moment she was afraid that they'd been watching her, and somehow seen her hide the journal and stone. To Linda's relief, suddenly her fingers touched the old paper and she brought them out. "They may have taken the sleigh," she said, "but they didn't get the journal or the stone this time."

"How in the world . . .?" Bronco began.

Linda explained as they all went back to the house, where Mr White went to call the sheriff to report the theft and the attack on Linda. "I didn't take the time to put them back in the sleigh, and I didn't want to leave them out in plain sight, so . . ."

"Lucky for us," Bob said, picking up the stone and smoothing it. "What's the design on this one, Linda? Is it similar to the other one?"

"I don't know, I . . ." Linda reached for the chain to bring out the first stone, which she wore constantly now. She found nothing. "It's gone!" she gasped. "The stone is gone!"

"The person who hit you must have taken it," Bronco said, coming to sit across the table from her.

"It was probably the same man who tried to get it on the lake," Bob agreed.

"Thank goodness you already figured out what it meant," Mrs White said, serving lunch. "Eat," she ordered. "The stew will warm you."

"The sheriff should be here by the time we finish lunch," John White said. "He'll want to know everything that happened."

Linda sighed. "It's too bad Rango and Chica can't talk," she observed. "They must have seen the thieves; I didn't."

Rango's bark announced the arrival of the sheriff just as Mrs White finished clearing away the dishes. Mr White went to greet him, introducing him to everyone while Mrs White offered him pie and coffee and Bronco pulled up a chair.

Sheriff Hoskins was a tall, stocky man in his forties with a friendly smile. "Now suppose someone tells me what has been going on around here," he began.

They all interrupted each other, describing everything that had happened in the past few days. The sheriff listened without comment till everyone fell silent.

"You have no idea who the thieves might be?" he asked.

They exchanged glances, then shook their heads.

"And you feel they're after the treasure?"

"What else could it be?" Linda asked, feeling guilty for not having been able to help more.

"The sleigh is a valuable vehicle," Sheriff Hoskins reminded them. "You did say that you were offered a great deal of money for it, didn't you, Linda?"

She nodded.

"The wall carving is quite valuable, too," Mrs White said. "Yet it was returned."

The sheriff sighed.

"They took my stone, too," Linda added. "That wouldn't have any value except as a key to the treasure."

"Neither would the journal," Bob contributed.

The sheriff got up. "I'll do what I can, but without a description . . . We'll make sure everyone keeps an eye out for the sleigh. That's one thing that will be easy to spot, anyway."

Mr White sighed. "I was afraid there wouldn't be much you could do," he admitted, "but I did want you to know what's going on, Hal. I want these people caught. I don't like what's happening. People breaking in, hurting my guests, stealing things."

"We'll do our best," the sheriff promised as he left. "I'll keep in touch."

Silence followed and Linda felt a sharp tide of depression sweeping over her. It all seemed so useless, she thought bitterly. The faceless people who were seeking the treasure seemed to have all the advantages. Then she remembered the journal and the stone and her spirits lifted—that was one advantage she'd managed to keep.

"It's time for you to go to bed, Linda," Doña told her sternly.

Linda smiled at her. "May I take the journal with me?" she asked.

"Of course you may," Mrs White said. "You have certainly earned the right to read it first. I just hope you find something in it that's worth all you've suffered."

"I just hope it will tell us what happened to Melanie," Linda replied.

The journal took up its narrative about a month after the last entry in the other book and continued on in much the same vein, chronicling the unhappy household that had lived under the homestead roof. Then the focus of the writing began to change and the subject was Calvin rather than Anne, Enos, and Melanie's parents.

I slip away as often as I can. The ride to the valley isn't a long one and I want to help Calvin all I can, since he is building our home there. I only wish that I could share my secret with Anne; but that grows more and more impossible since Father and Mr Howard have quarrelled so bitterly. If Father knew that I was even seeing Calvin Howard, he would lock me in my room, I know.

I keep hoping that Father will change his mind about Mr Howard so that I can start planning my wedding.

There's so much to be done and I'm sure that Anne would love to help, but she's so troubled by Father's treatment of Enos that I just can't burden her with another secret.

Linda read on, intrigued by the unfolding drama of the past, almost forgetting that her main purpose in reading the document was to discover clues about the treasure. She'd read more than half the pages without even finding a mention of the treasure or the black keys, when a tap on her door brought her mind back from the past. She called a friendly "Come in".

"I hope I didn't wake you," Bob said, coming in to sit on the side of her bed.

"I've been reading," Linda answered, "not sleeping."

"Learn anything?"

"Not about the treasure," Linda admitted. "Melanie hasn't even written about it."

"You mean there's nothing in this one either?" His tone reflected her feeling of despair.

"Well, I haven't finished it, but so far there is only one thing that sticks in my mind."

"What's that?"

"Let me read you something and see if it means the same thing to you that it did to me," Linda said, turning back a couple of pages.

The valley is just perfect. I don't miss having the lake nearby since there's a stream running through the whole property and Calvin is building our house next to it. There are several large meadows that he's fenced for our stock and several more that he'll plough for our crops. It won't be a large ranch like the one Father has, but it will be ours and I know we will be happy there.

"That's it?" he asked, frowning. "I don't understand."

"Don't you recognize the land description?" Linda inquired.

"The valley we saw from the ridge," he gasped, his eyes lighting up. "The one marked with the x on the stone."

Linda nodded. "That's what I thought."

"You think that's a clue?" he asked.

"The stones have to mean something," Linda reminded him.

"What does the second one have on it?" Bob inquired, picking it up off her nightstand.

Linda shrugged. "It's like the first one," she admitted. "Unless we can match it to what it is supposed to show, we'll never be able to figure it out."

Bob sighed. "I wonder how many more stones and journals are hidden in that sleigh."

"I keep wondering what the thief is doing with the sleigh," Linda murmured. "I mean, what if he chops it up looking for clues?"

Bob looked ill. "Do you really think he would?"

Linda could only shrug.

Bob got up. "Well, I'd better go feed the horses. Let me know if you find anything interesting in the journal."

"Oh, I will," Linda assured him, picking up the book. "I just hope it comes along pretty soon. I'm running out of entries."

Bob left and Linda settled back, reading on to the end of the journal. It was interesting, but not helpful. The treasure wasn't mentioned at all and neither were the black keys. It was as though Melanie had forgotten the whole thing in the magic of her love for Calvin Howard.

Linda shut the worn notebook and closed her eyes. Her excitement at finding the book and stone gave way to despair at having lost the sleigh. It seemed that nothing brought her any closer to solving the mystery of the treasure. Linda slept till Doña came in to tell her that dinner was ready.

"I'm so glad you're feeling better," Doña told her. "Did you know that they're forecasting snow for tonight?"

"Snow?" Linda swallowed a sigh. "But I wanted to go riding tomorrow."

"We'll talk about that later," Doña said, "after we're sure that your head is going to be all right."

Linda laughed. "I'm not sure how well it was working before I was hit," she teased. "If I'd been paying attention, I might have saved the sleigh."

"Well, I certainly . . ." Doña stopped as a pale Mrs White came through the door. "What is it, Beatrice?" she asked.

"That phone call," Mrs White began. "Oh, Roz,

94

Linda, that was our lawyer. He called to say that a claim has been filed against our land."

"A claim?" Doña gasped.

"Who'd do that?" Linda asked.

Mrs White's eyes were wide and unfocused as she looked at Linda. "He said that it was filed by the descendants of Melanie Davis Howard."

"Melanie's descendants?" Linda gasped, caught between happiness at the proof that the young girl who'd written the journal had been married to Calvin and shock that she or her descendants would suddenly come to claim their heritage.

"Is there anything in that journal about her marriage?" Beatrice White asked, her normal colour returning.

"Not about the marriage," Linda began, then told her what she'd read about Melanie's plans.

"That could be why she disappeared," Doña said when Linda finished. "Perhaps her father didn't make up with Mr Howard and she was forced to run away and get married."

"But if they planned to settle nearby, why wouldn't my mother have known?" Mrs White asked.

There wasn't any answer to that question, so Linda simply handed her the journal.

"Why do you think they would place a claim now?" Doña asked. "I mean, after so many years."

Mrs White frowned. "You don't think that they . . . well, that they have something to do with what has been happening to us recently?"

Linda hesitated for a moment, then nodded. "They would be the most likely ones to know about the sleigh and the treasure," she reminded them. "I mean, Melanie could have told them about everything."

"But why try to steal the sleigh?" Mrs White asked. "It would legally be half theirs, anyway. Mother told me that Grandfather's will left the land and everything to them both. She always considered herself simply a caretaker for Melanie's share, even though I believe my father finally took legal steps so that the business could be handled without any need for Melanie's signature."

"I guess you'll just have to wait and talk to them when they come to meet you," Doña suggested.

"Are they coming soon?" Linda asked.

"I have no idea when they might come," Mrs White answered, "but I doubt that it will be very soon. They didn't even give any names on the letter they sent our lawyer. They just said that they were going to institute a claim against the estate, and signed it as Melanie's descendants."

"Where was it sent from?" Linda asked, brushing her long black hair into order.

"It had a California postmark—somewhere in the Los Angeles area, I think—but no return address." Mrs White shook her head. "Now that I think about it, that sounds strange, doesn't it? I mean, how would someone all the way in Los Angeles be aware of us or our lawyer here in Lakeville?"

"You think that it could be a hoax?" Linda asked.

The woman shrugged. "I don't know what I think, but I'm not going to worry about it any more tonight. Come on along to dinner, Linda. Did anyone tell you that we're expecting more snow tonight?"

Dinner was a rather subdued meal and Linda felt no excitement when the promised storm arrived. She could think of only one thing: that the secluded valley would be buried under a white coat and she'd never be able to discover whether the second stone was the key to the mystery. She excused herself early, pleading her head ached. She lay staring at the ceiling for a long time.

In the morning, she woke to cloudy skies and a different kind of cold. Nearly a foot of new snow covered the rutted remains of earlier storms, and the scene outside looked like a Christmas card, all fresh and new.

"Want to go into town with us this afternoon?" Bob asked as they headed for the stable after they finished breakfast.

"What for?" Linda questioned, her thoughts on the distant valley.

"The Whites want to talk to their lawyer, and I'd like to see that letter myself. Maybe there is a clue in it."

"That's good thinking," Linda told him, "but you don't need my help."

"So what are you going to do?" Bob asked.

"I'd like to go through the journal again and I want to study the wall carving, to see if there are any other differences between it and the real sleigh." She sighed. "Just in case we ever find the sleigh again."

Bob looked at her oddly for a moment, then nodded. "I guess you are better off staying inside today," he said, "after what happened."

"I'm fine," Linda assured him. "I don't even have a headache this morning."

"You're lucky Rango was here," Bob told her. "You could have been in bad shape lying out in the snow without a coat."

Linda scratched behind the dog's ears. "That is another good reason for me to stay home today," she said. "I'll keep Rango and the horses company while you're all gone."

"I wish the weather hadn't changed," Bob complained. "We might not get to do much more riding while we're here if it doesn't clear up."

"We have to go to Melanie's valley," Linda protested.

"As soon as the sun comes out," Bob agreed as he unlocked the stable and they went in to feed the horses.

After lunch Linda watched everyone drive away with a pang of fear, remembering all too clearly what had happened to her yesterday. But she reminded herself that there wasn't anything left for the thieves to take—unless they knew about the stone and the second journal. And she was pretty sure they didn't—if they'd known, they would have taken them when they took the sleigh.

Unsure exactly what she was looking for, Linda picked up the journal and settled herself at the kitchen table. Her concentration lasted less than an hour. By then, a light wind had blown the clouds away and bright sunlight was spilling over the sparkling countryside.

Linda let Rango out and stood in the door of the service porch, savouring the fresh air, which seemed much warmer than it had been earlier. She looked at her watch and was surprised to find that it was still quite early, much too early for everyone to be returning from town.

She nibbled a finger, torn between an overwhelming desire to ride to the valley and a sure feeling that Bronco and Doña would be furious if she went alone. But the day was clear and beautiful, she reasoned, and it might not be so nice tomorrow.

Besides, it wasn't that far. She might even be able to get back before they did.

The temptation was too great. She changed into her heavy riding clothes, scribbled a note, then went out to saddle Chica. Rango followed at her heels, but when she led the filly out of the stable, she ordered the dog back inside.

"I can't let you come, boy," she told his accusing eyes. "Your paw is just healing nicely and that's too far for you to go."

Rango didn't look convinced, but he was too well-trained to make any objection when Linda shut him in the stable with Rocket. She mounted the excited filly and set off through the snow towards the trail to the valley.

The ride, though slightly longer than Linda remembered, was a pleasant one. Chica was full of energy after being in her stall all day yesterday. Linda reined in when she reached the ridge where she'd stopped before. This time she took out the second stone and compared it, not to the distant mountain skyline, but to the scene below. Her heartbeat quickened as she realized that she'd been right!

The marks on the stone weren't quite as correct as the first ones had been but this time she had to allow for the changes that time had brought about. Still, the stream was a dark path through the new snow, and most of the meadows were accurately carved into the stone's surface. The tiny x marked a spot near the smallest meadow and quite close to the stream.

"Well, Chica," Linda said, "shall we go down and explore?"

The filly danced forward, obviously eager to go on with the ride. Linda left the trail, urging the horse forward, but leaving the reins loose enough for Chica to pick her own way through the uncertain footing of the rough country.

It wasn't an easy descent, but the palomino was sure-footed and they reached the meadow without mishap. Linda hurried her across it and through the small belt of trees that protected the stream from the open area. Once there, she reined in and studied the ground.

At first it appeared to be featureless; then her eyes adjusted to the fluffy cover of the snow. She dismounted, picking her way across the snowy ground to where she'd noticed strange rises and ridges under their white coats. Chica followed her, watching with curious eyes as Linda uncovered a fallen log, several boulders, and at last what appeared to be the foundation of a building.

"This is it!" Linda crowed to the fascinated filly. "This has to be the house that Calvin was building for Melanie."

"And what does that mean?" Randy's voice seemed to come out of the wall of fir trees. Linda jumped with shock at the sound.

"What are you doing here?" she demanded.

"I was out riding and I saw you coming down here," Randy answered, emerging from between the trees. "I followed you."

"Why didn't you say something sooner?" Linda asked, playing for time, trying to think. She'd never liked or trusted Randy Fox, and now she had a chilling feeling that this meeting was far from accidental.

"I was curious," Randy admitted with a false smile. "What are you doing out exploring all by yourself, Linda?"

"I just thought Chica needed some exercise,"

Linda replied, hating the need to lie, but knowing that she couldn't trust him with the truth.

"So you rode over here, stopped on the ridge and looked around, then rode directly to this area?" His tone was mocking. "Oh, come now, Linda, we both know that you were looking for something, and from what you just said, you've found it."

Linda swallowed hard, realizing that Randy must have been following and watching her since she left the house. But what did it mean?

"Well, as a matter of fact, I was looking for this particular spot," she admitted, deciding to see what she could learn from him.

"Why? What is this place?" His interest was obvious, but she couldn't tell if it was rooted in more than natural nosiness.

"Don't you know?" she asked. "I thought since you lived around here, you might be able to tell me something about the valley."

His blue eyes changed and his expression became ugly. "I know that this land belongs to the Whites, but that's all." She could tell from his tone that he was lying.

Linda sighed, wishing that she could just mount Chica and ride away without saying anything further. But she had the distinct feeling that Randy wouldn't allow that. His big white horse would be a formidable match for the dainty filly, especially in this unfamiliar territory.

"What were you looking for?" Randy asked.

Linda tried to think of a believable story, but in the end she realized that it was hopeless. "I was looking for the homestead that Calvin Howard was building for Melanie Davis," she answered, deciding that the truth was the best answer.

"Melanie Davis never lived here," Randy stated, surprising her. "Everybody knows that she disappeared."

"What else does everybody know?" Linda asked, pleased at his response.

Randy coloured and his eyes avoided hers as he shrugged. "There was just a lot of talk when Mrs White told everybody about the sleigh and the journal you found in it. My family comes from this area and they knew all about the mighty Davis family and all the land they grabbed and held." There was a note of envy in his voice.

Linda said nothing, choosing instead to brush a little more snow off the stone foundation. She was very conscious of the stone in her jacket pocket and could only hope that Randy had been too far away to see it when she'd followed its guidelines.

"So what do you care about this old place?" Randy asked, breaking into her thoughts.

"Well, like you said, I found the journal and I read it. I sort of feel like I knew Melanie Davis, so I got curious about the house that she was to live in and . . ." Linda stopped, realizing that she was talking about the second journal and not the first.

"There wasn't anything about a house here in the journal," Randy said. Then he, too, stopped and gulped, guilt spreading over his features like a stain. "I mean, I heard that . . ."

"You took the journal," Linda gasped, shocked rather than surprised.

"No, I didn't. I just . . . It wasn't me." Randy stepped back from her.

"What else did you take?" Linda asked, pressing her advantage. "Did you steal the original sleigh carving, Randy? You would have known about that,

103

too. And what about the sleigh? Are you the one who hit me yesterday?"

"Hit you?" The utter shock on his face was her answer. "Who hit you?" he demanded.

Linda stopped, suddenly sorry that she hadn't just taken her knowledge and fled back to the house while Randy was still floundering in his guilty confusion. She took a couple of backward steps of her own, moving towards Chica.

"What are you talking about?" Randy asked. "I didn't know that anyone had hit you. When did that happen?"

Linda glared at him, her momentary fear turning to anger. "I think you know more about it than you show. Who hit me, Randy? Who stole the sleigh and the black stone? Who is claiming the Whites' land?"

His silence was her answer, that and the confusion in his face. Linda hesitated only a moment, then caught the patient filly's reins and vaulted into the saddle. She turned Chica around just as she felt the first icy blast of wind. It was so hard it nearly swept her out of the saddle.

"Linda, wait!" Randy's voice came clearly over the wind, but even as he shouted at her, he disappeared behind a cloud of white.

For a heartbeat, Linda was too stunned to move. The sky had been clear; now the air was full of snow. Chica shifted under her, plainly wanting direction, perhaps as frightened as she was by the violence of the wind and snow.

A dark shape materialized out of the snow and she felt the reins jerked from her suddenly icy fingers. Chica began to move forward and there was nothing Linda could do but cling to her back, shivering and terrified.

It was like being trapped in a nightmare. The wind grew steadily colder till the snowflakes felt like bits of ice being driven into Linda's body. She longed to simply clap her heels into Chica's sides and race away from the nearly invisible rider ahead of them, but she knew that it would be futile. She might escape Randy, but the storm would trap her much more effectively.

Suddenly, the onslaught of the storm lessened slightly and she realized that they had reached the forest and were climbing slowly through the trees. The wind raged viciously against the pines and the snow was rapidly building deep drifts which the horse had to flounder through.

Then, without warning, Chica simply stopped. Linda was too cold and frightened to move. She could see little beyond the dim shapes of the trees and the pale bulk of the horse ahead of her. She wasn't even aware of Randy till she felt his hands forcing her feet out of the stirrups and pulling her off Chica.

"What are you doing?" she demanded.

"Getting you to safety," he answered. "You have to lead your horse, so follow me." He handed her Chica's reins, then disappeared again as the storm raged more violently. After a moment, the big white horse began to move and Linda forced her numb feet to follow him.

Randy led them through the snowstorm . . .

Fortunately, the trek was a short one. The yawning darkness of a cave welcomed them and the moment she stepped inside, Linda felt relief as the wind was cut off and only a small amount of snow flowed in behind them. She stopped as soon as Chica was inside, afraid to move further in the darkness, no longer sure where Randy was.

A light flared in the darkness ahead, throwing wild shadows on the damp, rocky walls. Linda shrank back against Chica's warm, wet side, drawing strength from the filly's nearness. The light became the steady glow of a lantern and the shadows resolved themselves into Randy and his horse.

"Where are we?" Linda managed, her voice making a strange, squeaky echo in the rocky chamber.

"This is just a cave," Randy answered. "We are about a mile from where we were. It's the closest place I could think of."

Linda ran a shaking hand over her face, which was very wet and cold. Her body heat was starting to melt the snow that had been crusted on her eyelashes and hair by the driving wind. "What happened out there?" she asked. "It was such a beautiful day. Where did the snow come from?"

"It was a ground blizzard." Randy took Chica's reins and led her up beside his horse. "Last night's snow getting rearranged by the wind. It happens sometimes."

Linda peered outside, shivering in the icy cold. "How long will it last?" she asked.

Randy came forward, his arms full of wood. "It could last till nightfall, or it could stop any time," he answered. "Meanwhile, I'll build a fire so we can warm up. That wind is cold."

"You mean we're trapped here till the wind drops?" Linda gasped.

"There's no way we could find our way home through that," Randy answered calmly. "It's just lucky that I remembered this cave and that it was close enough for me to find it."

Linda nodded, suddenly aware that she might well owe her life to this young man. "I couldn't see a thing," she admitted.

Randy lit the fire and made sure it was burning well before he turned to her. "Now we'll have time to finish our conversation," he observed.

Linda took a step backward, not anxious to pursue the conversation even though she was aware that she'd uncovered guilt on Randy's part. "What is this cave?" she asked, leaving the fire and going back to where the horses patiently stood as the melting snow dripped off their hides. "I mean, was it a mine or what?"

"I don't know," Randy replied. "It's just a big cave. I've played here since I was a kid. We used to picnic on rainy days, and some of our twilight rides come here. That's why there's always a supply of dry wood, a lantern, and even a tin of crackers and a couple of cans of pop stored here."

"Home away from home," Linda teased, his words so ordinary that they made her feel easier. "How deep is this, anyway?" She picked up the lantern and started past the horses.

"Hey, don't go back there," Randy called, and she heard his footsteps on the stony floor.

Startled by his tone, she dodged past the big gelding and held the lantern high to illuminate the shadows beyond the horses.

"Linda, please . . ." Randy let the words trail off, then sighed.

108

Linda said nothing; she was too shocked. The light of the lantern reflected dully off the carved surface of the wooden sleigh.

"I . . . uh . . . can explain," Randy began.

Linda turned to face him. "You stole it?"

Randy squirmed a little then shook his head. "I knew it was stolen, that's all. And I helped hide it here. I didn't know you'd been hurt, Linda. I wouldn't have let that happen."

Linda went back and examined the sleigh, feeling relieved that it was still safe. "What are you going to do with the sleigh, Randy?" she asked.

"I'm not going to do anything with it." He evaded her eyes.

"What do *they* want with it then?" Linda persisted. "Why do they keep stealing things? What do they expect to find?"

"Proof of ownership," Randy answered.

"Ownership of what?" Linda was puzzled.

Randy finally faced her. "Half of everything," he answered. "They want to take half of the land that the Whites have here and turn it into a resort. It'll be great and I'll be manager."

"Manager?" Linda couldn't hide her doubts.

"I'll be ready by the time they get it built," Randy protested. "I'm going to college next year and I'll take management courses. They promised that I'd have full control once it was built."

Linda just looked at him, seeing in his eyes that he was beginning to doubt the promises. She could almost feel sorry for him. "Why do they need the sleigh?" she asked. "Mrs White already told my grandparents that the ranch was left to both her mother and her Aunt Melanie. All they would have to do is prove that they are Melanie's descendants."

Randy said nothing, but merely glared at her, then returned to the fire. Linda waited for several minutes, then sighed and went forward to sit on a chunk of pine near the fire.

"You found another notebook, didn't you?" Randy asked.

"Does it matter?" Linda retorted, her anger burning.

"Does it tell you where the treasure is?" Randy still didn't look at her.

"Why should I tell you?" Linda inquired tartly. "So you can inform your friends and they can knock me out and leave me to freeze again?"

"Is that what they did?" Randy looked honestly horrified.

Linda nodded. "If it hadn't been for Rango lying down beside me, I probably would have frozen solid." She actually had her doubts that it would have been that serious, but she did remember the cold and the pain. She lifted her hand to touch the sore spot at the base of her skull.

"I didn't know about it, Linda," Randy said softly.

Linda watched him for several minutes, not sure whether she could believe him. Then she shivered slightly. "Is there anything in this cave that I could use to wipe Chica down?" she asked. "If this storm ever stops, I don't want her out in the cold still wet from the snow."

Randy shrugged. "Look in the corner by the sleigh. There might be a couple of burlap bags, unless someone else carried them out."

Linda left his morose company gladly, preferring to spend her time with the horses. She located the bags without difficulty and was soon rubbing first Chica, then the white gelding. She was relieved to find that Chica seemed quite well and content, unaffected by the terrible time in the blizzard.

Linda was still petting the filly when she sensed a change. She looked around, aware of a silence much deeper than she'd heard before. Her eyes were drawn immediately to the mouth of the cave, and she gasped at the sight of slanting sunlight gleaming on great mounds of sparkling snow.

"Looks like the storm is over," Randy said, getting to his feet.

"You mean we can go home now?" Linda asked, her heart pounding with excitement.

"Let's get the horses," Randy answered, hurrying past her to lead the big gelding out.

Linda went back to Chica, then slowed as she led the filly by the fire. Randy was waiting just outside the cave, already mounted. "Aren't you going to put out the fire?" Linda asked, her years of camping on her mind.

"Let me hold Chica," he said, "you can kick a little snow over it."

"Well, I don't . . ." Linda began, but before she could go on, the reins were jerked from her hand and Randy was moving away.

"I can't let you go home, Linda," he shouted over his shoulder. "It's too far for you to walk so don't try it. You'll be safe and warm enough here if you keep the fire going, and you can eat the food in the back."

"You can't leave me!" Linda screamed, running after him. "Chica!"

The filly tried to turn, fighting Randy's hold on her bridle, squealing in anger when Randy spurred the gelding ahead, dragging her after him. Linda called her name again, but there was no stopping them, and Chica's golden body disappeared into the trees.

Linda followed their tracks for another few feet, but the going was slippery and difficult as she ploughed into a drift and nearly went down. She was panting for breath as she straightened up and looked around.

There was sunlight, but the rays were slanting, and a glance at her watch told there was less than an hour and a half till sunset—barely long enough for her to ride back home through the snowdrifts—nowhere near enough time for her to walk that distance. Sobs swelled in her throat as she heard Chica's distant whinny and knew that the filly was still trying to return to her.

Shivering as the icy air reached her, she turned back, picking her way carefully through the drifts, heading for the safety of the cave. Bob, Bronco, and Mr White would come looking for her once they found the note and the storm was over, she silently assured herself.

A heavy depression settled over her like a chilling blanket. Bob would know about the valley, but nothing else. They wouldn't know where to look once they came, and the ground blizzard would have covered any trail she and Chica had made. There was no way they could find her, not here—and no way that she could go anywhere else.

Linda sank down on the stump that she'd left earlier, not sure what she was going to do, wanting mostly to cry in her frustration and growing fear. Finally, however, her sense of survival revived and she got to her feet, determined not to be defeated by despair. There was always tomorrow, she reminded herself. If she left here at sunrise, she'd be able to walk to the Whites' before noon.

Exploring the cave occupied her time as the day

waned. She found the woodpile and carried some of it to the front to add to the fire. She checked the lantern and assured herself that it held enough oil for the night. The crackers and pop weren't exactly a nourishing meal, but they stilled the rumbling in her stomach temporarily.

Finally, Linda carried the lantern to the rear of the cave and stood looking at the sleigh. "Do you have any more secrets?" she asked the panels as they seemed to move in the flickering light of the lantern.

She began a methodical search, checking first one side, then the other, and moving to the inside of the sleigh to check the board beneath the second seat, but with no success. Finally, weary and feeling defeated, she moved to the rear of the sleigh and the final carving.

Looks familiar, Linda observed to herself as she studied the graceful skaters and the familiar shoreline of the lake. The scene could have been carved from either of the skating parties they'd had since their arrival.

But did it hide something? She began moving her fingers lazily over everything, touching any surface that might hide a secret panel, running her fingers carefully under any carved area that could hide a lever.

It seemed to be a useless task, and she was almost ready to give up, when something under the carved bulge of a rocky projection clicked and the third panel swung quietly open. Linda filled the dim cavern with her excited laughter as she took out the contents.

Her hands unclasped a third stone, this one also pierced at one end, and strangely shaped like a hook with an odd pattern of ridges on the other end. It, too, had been carved, though the light was too poor for her to see what was cut into its black surface.

This time there was no notebook, only a single folded sheet and an envelope addressed to Anne Landsburg. Linda sighed, carrying everything to the front of the cave where she could enjoy the warmth of the fire while she tried to read the final message from Melanie Davis.

The date was about two months after the end of the other journal, and the handwriting seemed hurried, almost scribbled.

I'm hiding this and the final key in the last of the secret compartments, for tonight I leave this unhappy place and I doubt that I will ever return. Calvin's father has forbidden our marriage and threatened to tell my father of our plans, so we will leave them to their foolish battle.

Once we are settled on the West Coast, I'll write Anne and tell her what I've done. She'll be amused to know that Father's treasure is hidden in our never-to-be house. The last key will guide her to it and open the hiding place. My only sorrow is that I dare not tell her now, before I leave. I can only hope that my letter will be enough for her to forgive all my deceptions.

If things go wrong, perhaps she will find one of these journals and then the others. I know nothing else to do, no other place to hide them, for no one must know our plans.

There was a slight blot at the bottom, as though she might have been planning to write more and been interrupted. Linda turned the sheet over, hoping to find more. But there was nothing—just the envelope, which was sealed, and the third black stone.

She started to rub the stone, to try to clear the carving, when a distant sound reached her ears. It was a motor. Joy swept over her and she started to run to the mouth of the cave. Then she remembered the yellow snowmobile and fear gripped her.

Not taking time to think, Linda ran to the back of the cave and opened the panel, slipping the sheet, envelope, and both stones into the compartment. She closed it and made her way cautiously back to the curve, rounding it just as the motor snarled to a halt beyond the fire.

Linda stood quietly, hoping she was in the shadows. Luckily, she'd left the lantern near the fire and had returned her discoveries to their hiding place in nearly complete darkness. For a moment, there was just silence beyond the crackling fire. Then a man stepped inside.

"Linda Craig," he called. "Are you in here, Linda?"

Linda put her hand to her lips so that he wouldn't hear her gasp as she recognized both his face and his voice. He was the man from the parade, the mysterious collector who'd offered to buy the sleigh.

"Come on out, Linda," the man continued. "I know you're still in here and there's no place to hide."

She swallowed hard, aware that he spoke the truth. Except for the sleigh, there was nothing to conceal her and nowhere that she could run. The cavern narrowed to nothing just a few feet beyond the sleigh, and the man stood in the only exit.

"Don't make me leave you here all night, Linda," the man called. "You won't like it when it gets below zero and the fire dies out."

Linda took a deep breath and stepped out of the shadows. "Who are you, and what do you want?" she demanded, doing her best not to let her fear show in her voice.

"Well, well, so you were hiding back there." He sounded pleased. "You're lucky I didn't ignore what Randy said and leave you here. Maybe a night in the cold would make you a little less sassy."

"Like hitting me over the head and leaving me out in the snow did?" The words were out before she could stop them.

"Doesn't look like I hurt you any more than I did that first afternoon on the lake," he drawled after a moment. "So what did you find in the sleigh?"

"Find?" Linda sounded as innocent as she could, but she was too frightened to be convincing.

"Randy said you were poking around in the valley, so you must have found something else. Suppose you just be a good girl and tell me what it was."

"I'm not going to tell you anything," Linda said, lifting her chin firmly.

He laughed cruelly. "You have more courage than most little girls would," he told her. "Not that it is going to do you any good. I want to know what you found in the sleigh, and I mean to have an answer."

Linda said nothing, clamping her lips together, and hoping desperately that he'd simply leave her alone. If he went away, she reasoned, she could wait till morning, then be gone by the time he returned. A few moments later Linda realized that was too easy to be true.

The man glared at her for several minutes and she endured his angry gaze without wilting. Finally, he simply shrugged and began kicking snow onto her fire.

"Don't do that," she cried, too frightened to keep quiet.

"Why not?" he asked. "Don't you want to stay here without it?"

Linda bit her lip. "If I freeze to death, you'll never find out what I know," she warned him.

His lean features drew together in an ominous frown. Then to her surprise, he laughed. "You are a tough one," he commented as the fire sizzled and steamed, then settled into damp death. "But as it happens, you aren't staying here, anyway."

"You're going to take me home?" Linda asked.

"Fat chance."

"Then I'm not going with you." Linda retreated towards the shadows, not sure what she was doing, but afraid to go with this cruel stranger.

He was after her in a flash, and his hands were quick and strong as he tied her wrists together with a soft cord. Linda tried to kick him, but his slap stopped her. "You behave," he warned her. "I don't want to hurt you, but time seems to be running out and I want that treasure."

"Well, I don't have it," Linda answered with angry honesty.

"But I'll bet you know where it is, don't you?"

She didn't answer, and luckily, he didn't seem to notice as he turned out the lantern and led her outside to the waiting snowmobile. He put her on it, then sat behind her, keeping her still as he guided the machine over the drifts and between the trees till they reached the open sweep of the meadow.

"Where are you taking me?" she shouted above the snarl of the machine.

"You'll find out," was his only answer.

Frightened, but determined, Linda tried to watch where they were going, to note landmarks, but the darkness was nearly complete and the single headlight of the snowmobile revealed little beyond the path they were following. She could only hope

118

Linda fought to escape . . .

that the track would remain until morning and perhaps guide Bob and Bronco to wherever she was being taken.

Linda and the man seemed to be riding forever. Then, suddenly, they left the forest and she could see a small cabin ahead of them, lights gleaming from its windows. The man stopped in front of the door, which opened at once to reveal a very tense-looking Randy.

"Take her inside, Randy," he ordered. "I'll put the snowmobile in the shed with your horse for now."

Randy's hands were gentle as he helped her off the snowmobile, and she followed him into the cabin without a word. Only when he closed the door against the icy air did she look at him.

"How could you?" she demanded.

"I couldn't let you spend the night in that cave," Randy said. "You'd have frozen to death before morning."

"You could have called the Whites and told them where I was."

"I had to tell Gabe first. He'll leave if you just tell him what you found in the sleigh."

"Leave?" Linda stared at him. "I thought he was going to take the land and build a resort for you to run."

"Of course I am," the man said from the doorway as he came in, stamping the snow from his boots. "A wonderful resort."

His tone was mocking and Linda could see that Randy didn't believe him. "He just wants the treasure," she told Randy, not looking at the man again. "There isn't going to be any resort. If he was really a relative, all he'd have to do is talk to Mrs

White. She'd love to know what happened to her aunt."

Randy said nothing, but his expression was bleak. Linda turned her attention to the man. "Who are you, anyway?" she asked.

"You are a nosy kid," he replied, then sighed, "but I guess it doesn't matter now, does it? You know more than you should already."

"His name is Gabe Ingram," Randy supplied.

The man made a mocking bow in Linda's direction. "Gabe Ingram, collector of art treasures and antiques, at your service." Then he looked at Randy. "Did you fix something to eat?" he asked.

Randy nodded. "I opened a couple of cans of spaghetti."

Ingram sighed. "I suppose I might as well untie you," he told Linda. "There's nowhere for you to run in these mountains, and you can't eat with your hands tied."

"I would like to go home," Linda said coldly. Her fear was fading slightly since Randy was here, too. Though he'd been no friend to her, she sensed that he was rapidly losing any regard he had for Gabe Ingram, and she thought he might be willing to help her escape if Ingram continued to treat him the way he had been.

"Well, you can forget that," Ingram growled. "You're not leaving till you tell me where the treasure is hidden."

"I don't know where it is," Linda stated honestly, not adding that she had the clues to find it but hadn't had the opportunity to use them yet.

"Well, you'd better figure it out," Ingram snarled, "'cause I'm not letting you go till I have the treasure."

"Do you know what it is?" Linda asked, changing her tactics.

His eyes narrowed as he glared at her. "Don't you?"

She shook her head. "Even Mrs White doesn't know."

"See, I told you," Randy said and was rewarded with a cold glare.

"You've told me a lot of things," Ingram snapped, "and most of them haven't been right."

"I did the best I could," Randy protested. "And you lied to me. You never told me about the treasure till I read the journal myself. Then you said . . ."

"Shut up and eat." Ingram ladled the spaghetti into bowls and put out bread and butter.

"How did you learn about the treasure?" Linda asked Ingram, her curiosity aroused.

He glared at her for a moment, then shrugged. "I guess it doesn't matter now," he said. "I read about it in the journals of Melanie Davis Howard."

"You have her journals?" Linda frowned, thinking of the second one she'd taken from the sleigh before it was stolen and the final sheet that she'd hidden just before Ingram found her in the cave.

"Lots of them," Ingram answered, waving a hand at a box on the far side of the cabin. He laughed without humour. "I bought an antique chest at an auction a couple of months ago and when I discovered it had a false bottom, there they were. I almost burned the blasted books, and the way things have been going . . ."

"Where is she now?" Linda asked, ignoring the rest of his words. "Where is Melanie?"

Ingram looked as though he was going to say something unkind, then he sighed. "Buried in some churchyard in Australia, I guess," he said. "The chest was sold by her heirs, as far as I know. I picked it up from a dealer who imported a whole boatload of antiques from Australia."

"Was she happy there?" Linda asked, remembering the sadness of the final entry she'd read. "In Australia, I mean."

"What do I care?" Ingram roared. "What's with the dumb questions? I want to know where the treasure is hidden. Now tell me."

"I don't know," Linda answered. "You're the one who has all the journals."

"I know that the sleigh has all the answers," Ingram mumbled with a mouthful of food. "She wrote that often enough. But she never said where they were hidden."

"Did you find the rest of the clues, Linda?" Randy asked.

"I found another journal, but it doesn't tell where the treasure is," Linda replied, playing for time.

"What did it tell you?" Ingram asked.

"About Calvin Howard."

Ingram laughed nastily. "The man who dragged her halfway around the world because he fought with his old man?" He shook his head. "She should have left old Calvin here and taken the treasure with her. Probably would have done more for her."

Linda said nothing, but cast a longing glance at the big box across the room, hoping that she'd have a chance to read the journals and knowing how much they would mean to Mrs White.

Thinking of the Whites made her remember her position here, and she felt a chill of fear. If only she could get on Chica and . . .

Chica! In all the confusion, she realized that she hadn't thought about the filly since Ingram had brought her here. Linda put her fork down. "Did you feed Chica?" she asked Randy.

"Huh?" Randy just looked at her, his face blank.

"My horse," Linda continued. "Did you feed her? Where is she?"

There was a long silence while Randy evaded her eye and Ingram glared at them both. Finally, Ingram spoke. "What horse is she talking about?" he demanded.

Randy said nothing, squirming in his chair, poking at his food, but not lifting anything to his mouth.

"Where is Chica, Randy?" Linda asked, containing a scream only by a tremendous effort of will. "Is she out in that shed with your horse?"

Randy didn't lift his head; he just put down his fork and continued to stare at his plate. Linda looked at Ingram. "Is she out there?" she asked.

Ingram was frowning now, his eyes showing confusion mixed with anger. "There's only one horse in that shed," he answered, then shifted his gaze to Randy. "What horse is she talking about?" he asked again, his tone deadly.

"I don't know, Gabe." The words were almost a whisper.

"Where is she?" Linda screamed, her fury rising with her fear. "Randy, what did you do with Chica?"

"I got rid of her," Randy snapped, finally looking up. "She fought every step of the way, even reared and hit me with a front hoof." He stopped for a moment, looking defiant and frightened at the same time. Linda wanted to reach across the table and shake him, to force him to go on; but she couldn't move. She was too afraid of what he might be going to say.

"I had to let the horse go, Gabe," Randy whined. "She jerked the reins out of my hands and took off. I couldn't get her and . . ."

Linda let her breath out slowly, relieved that he hadn't injured the filly.

"Now what happens?" Ingram asked.

"She'll freeze to death," Randy answered. "She's a fancy stable horse and there's no way she could get back to Whites' from up here. We don't have to worry about her."

Linda's joy faded as she realized the truth of the words. At home on the Rancho del Sol, Chica would have been perfectly safe; but here in the unfamiliar mountains and snow, the frightened and confused filly might do almost anything. Linda closed her eyes, picturing Chica floundering in the drifted snow, falling, slowly freezing.

"You're sure she couldn't get home?" Ingram asked again.

Randy grinned at him. "Nah, we were pretty close to here when she got loose, and it's a long way back to the Whites'. She was half-crazy from fighting me."

Ingram didn't look convinced, but he asked no more questions, and just stared at Randy for quite a while, then shifted his gaze back to Linda. "If you don't tell me where the treasure is, I think I'll do the same with you," he said. "Take you out and dump you in the snow. By the time they find you and your horse, it'll just look like a riding accident."

"You'll never find the treasure if you do that," Linda warned, too worried about Chica to really care what he threatened.

"Then you do know where it is!" Ingram jumped to his feet, dumping over his chair in a crash that shook the entire room.

"No," Linda gasped, her attention brought back to the moment. "No, I don't know where it is, but there . . . I found the second journal and I know there are more in the sleigh. I might have found it if you hadn't stolen the sleigh."

Ingram's eyes narrowed. He seemed to be thinking, then he nodded as though he'd made a decision. He turned to Randy. "Finish your food and get out of here," he said. "Your folks will think you're lost."

"What about Linda?" Randy asked, his concerned gaze resting on her.

"Don't worry about her," Ingram told him.

Randy didn't argue. Gulping down his food, he pulled on his heavy clothes without even looking her way. He disappeared through the door, leaving her alone with Gabe Ingram. She put down her fork and looked at him, very frightened.

"Are you going to tell me where the treasure is?" Ingram asked, his face cold and hard.

"I can't tell you what I don't know," Linda responded, doing her best to hide her fear.

Ingram stared at her for several minutes, then nodded. "Maybe you need some time to think it over," he observed. "How would you like to spend the night alone here?"

"I want to go home," Linda stated as firmly as she could.

"That's too bad." He got to his feet and picked up

his heavy jacket. "You're going to stay here till you tell me where the treasure is, so if you want to get home, you'd better figure it out."

He went to the door, then turned to look at her, waiting for her to say something. For a moment Linda considered telling him everything she'd learned. If she did and she got home, she could start a search for Chica and . . .

"I'll be back in the morning to see if you've remembered anything," Ingram said, his face mean. "Just don't try to leave here, or you'll freeze to death just like your horse."

Linda said nothing, his eyes telling her that he wouldn't take her home even if she could tell him what he wanted to know. He couldn't afford to let her go now that she knew so much. She turned her back, not even watching as he went out and closed the door behind him. She was alone once again.

Escape

Linda didn't move till she heard the snarl of the snowmobile as it started. Her stiff back suddenly slumped and she buried her face in her hands. The Whites and her family would be so worried about her and Chica . . . What had happened to Chica? Was Randy right? Would she freeze to death or would she perhaps return to the shelter of the cave?

A ray of hope touched her at that thought. Chica was an intelligent horse and she'd remember that the cave was warm and dry. But was it? The fire had been dead when they left, and the cold of the night . . .

The lonely whinny seemed to be a part of her frightening thoughts at first. Then suddenly Linda gasped and ran to the door, not caring that the cold swept in when she opened it. The whinny came again!

"Chica!" Linda pulled on her jacket and boots and raced out into the crystal-clear air. For a moment she just stood on the step of the small cabin looking around, trying to locate the source of the whinnies. "Chica, where are you?" she called.

The whinny shattered the air and Linda followed the sound around the side of the cabin and into the shed area. Chica stood there in the meagre shelter, shivering, her pretty head hanging.

"Oh, Chica!" Linda ran to her, throwing her arms around the filly's neck, hugging her with relief. "I thought you were dead," she whispered into the wet, snowy mane.

Chica nickered, but continued to shiver.

Linda looked around the stable, seeing the impossibility of leaving Chica there. The door was missing and there was no glass in the single window. It offered a roof and walls, but no real protection. Left here, she was sure that Chica would never make it through the cold night ahead.

"Come on, baby," she urged, reaching for the bridle reins and discovering that one had been broken, perhaps when Chica caught it on something or stepped on it when she was escaping from Randy's hold. "I'm taking you inside."

Chica followed her without resistance, not even shying when one of the stirrups banged against the doorjamb. Once inside with the door closed, Linda stepped back to look at her filly in the light. What she saw made her heart ache with fear.

Chica's body was ridged with frost and she was shivering violently. The saddle showed marks of contact either with the ground or with trees. There were scrapes, scratches, and cuts on Chica's shoulders and haunches.

Shaking with anger at what Randy had done, Linda stripped off the saddle. She took the sheet from the cot in the corner and used it to rub the filly dry, then put the blanket from the cot over Chica.

"You just rest," Linda told her palomino. "I'll go out and see if those awful people left any food for you in the shed."

The night seemed colder as she went outside and she shuddered to think what would have happened to Chica if she hadn't come to the cabin. Did Chica know I was here? she wondered. Or had she simply stayed in the vicinity because of Randy's horse being there? She shook her head, realizing that it didn't matter. Chica was safe and warm now; that was the important thing.

The shed contained a half bale of poor hay and a bag of horse pellets. Linda broke off a fair-sized flake of hay, then located a bucket for water and put the pellets in the bucket to carry into the cabin.

When she opened the door, Chica lifted her head, her interest relieving much of Linda's worry. It was, she knew, a sign of recovery. She spread the hay out on the discarded sheet in front of Chica, then poured out a pile of the pellets before going to the kitchen pump to fill the bucket with water.

Chica watched her at first, but soon the sounds of her chewing filled the small cabin. Linda sank down at the table again, watching the horse, content just to have her safe and warm in the cabin with her.

There was little to do besides wait. She placed another log on the fire and, once the shivering stopped, took the blanket off Chica.

Linda looked thoughtfully across the now crowded room at the box. Should she get out the journals? Weariness swept over her like a tide and she knew she couldn't even begin to concentrate on them. Too much had happened and there was still tomorrow to worry about. She looked at her watch and was startled to find that it was only eight-thirty.

"I guess we'll have to wait till morning," she told Chica. "Then we'll try to get out of here and back to the Whites'. I hope you can find the way, Chica. I certainly don't know where we are."

Chica nickered softly, then sighed, sounding quite content with her rescue.

"I suppose you like being a house horse," Linda chuckled, going to the filly's side to give her a few pats before she picked up the single blanket.

130

Wrapping it tightly around herself, she lay down on the cot. "Don't get too used to it," she teased as the filly nuzzled her cheek. "Doña would never agree to it."

Chica, apparently satisfied that all was well, calmly folded her slender legs and lay down on the sheet. In a moment, they were both sound asleep, too tired to worry about anything.

The tickling on her cheek was like a kitten's paw. Linda wiggled, trying to move away, but the tickling moved with her and she was dimly conscious of warm breath on her face. She moved again, lifting her hand to . . . Her fingers found the velvety skin of a horse's muzzle.

Linda opened her eyes, aware of a number of things all at the same time. She was in an unfamiliar bed and Chica was nuzzling her; the air she was breathing was surprisingly cold; and when she looked around, the room was dark. Memory rushed over her and she sat up abruptly, causing the filly to shy slightly.

"Whoa, girl," Linda said, automatically reaching out to soothe the palomino as she peered around, trying to make sense out of the darkness. The lantern had gone out while she slept and the fire in the fireplace was now barely glowing embers, which explained the chill in the room. Shivering, Linda went to add wood to the embers and was relieved when the fire blazed up once again.

In the firelight, she was able to read her watch and to see that it was about six in the morning. "I suppose you were looking for breakfast," she told the filly as she searched the kitchen cabinet for candles and food. She lit a fat candle, then poured out the remaining horse pellets for Chica.

131

While the filly crunched happily, she warmed the leftover spaghetti and ate the bread that remained from last night's meal. It wasn't exactly a routine breakfast, but it seemed better than the single can of pork and beans that sat on the shelf. "I think I'll complain to our host," she murmured as she swallowed the food. "The least he could have left is some bacon and eggs."

Chica snorted, pawing at the sheet in an attempt to track down a pellet that had disappeared in the folds. Linda laughed at her.

"Not up to your standards of food either, eh?" she said, getting up to find the pellet and feed it to her. "Maybe we should just pack up and go home, what do you think?"

Chica nodded her golden head happily in response to Linda's cue.

Linda went to the window and peered out. The sun hadn't risen yet and she had a feeling that it was very cold, but the sky was paling and, thanks to the snow and the clear sky, she could see the shadowed forest.

Linda nibbled at her lower lip, wondering what she should do. She was anxious to be on her way, yet she didn't want to leave too early and risk the most intense cold. Still, to stay too long was to invite disaster of another kind—if Gabe Ingram should return and find them in the cabin, she had no doubt that they would both be in danger.

Linda turned back to study her horse, and felt better. Chica seemed fine, showing no ill effects from nearly freezing the night before. Even the scratches on her haunches now looked superficial. Her coat gleamed in the flickering light of the fire and she was still sniffing around seeking more food.

"I hope you have the instincts of a homing pigeon, Chica," she told the filly as she picked up the saddle blanket and put it on her sleek back. "I have no idea where we are."

Chica nuzzled her as she lifted the saddle into place, standing quietly while Linda tightened the cinch. "Maybe we can follow the tracks of the snowmobile," Linda suggested. "Ingram must have gone to a road when he left here."

Once the horse was saddled and ready, Linda donned her parka and boots, then paused to take a last look around. She was just ready to open the door when she caught a glint of something shiny on the top of the box of journals. Curious, she went over to investigate.

The black stone lay on top of the first journal that Linda had found, and the gold chain glittered in the dancing light from the fireplace. Smiling, Linda picked it up and put it on, pleased to feel the weight of the stone against her throat once again.

"Too bad we don't have the saddlebags," she observed to Chica. "We could take all the journals with us, too."

She put out the fire so that the cabin would not be in any danger, then opened the door. Cold air rushed in and she shivered, pitying any creature that had been outside through the night. Chica snorted as she plunged down the step and into the snow. Linda mounted quickly, holding the single rein firmly as she looked around.

Hoofprints and runner tracks from the snowmobile led off in the same direction, but Linda hesitated, aware from the iciness of the morning that she couldn't afford to follow a false trail. Chica pulled at the bit, snorting and dancing a little in her eagerness.

133

"Okay, okay, you win," Linda told her, loosening her hold on the single rein. "You pick the trail."

Chica trotted off obediently, heading into the trees with a confidence that Linda was far from sharing. The morning stillness was almost eerie, and the plumes of their breath testified to the cold that the rising sun seemed unable to penetrate.

Time inched by. They crossed and recrossed the lines of the snowmobile runners and the line of hoofprints that Linda assumed belonged to Randy's big gelding, but she saw nothing else. No familiar landmark appeared out of the shadows or glinted on a snowswept ridge. Mountains reared all around her, primitive and forbidding, as clouds came to hide the bright blue of the sky and the wind began to rise.

"I hope you know where you're going, Chica," Linda told the tiring filly as they negotiated still another deep ridge of drifted snow. "I think it's going to storm again and I sure don't want to be caught in it this time."

Chica's golden ears turned back to listen to her voice, but there was no hesitation in her pace as she climbed towards the crest of still another ridge. Linda lifted her single rein as they reached the top, wanting to look around for a moment to try to discover where they were.

Chica stopped, but her head was up and her ears were pricked forward so sharply the tips nearly touched. She whinnied, loud and long, the sound echoing in the snowy stillness. Almost at once, there was a reply. Linda's heart lifted as she saw two familiar mounted figures break out of the trees below and realized that she was looking down on the secluded valley that she and Bob had discovered on the Saddle Club ride.

Chica needed no urging to race down the steep hill towards Bob and Bronco. Slipping and sliding in the treacherous footing, she reached them in a cloud of swirling snow. For a moment, Linda was too overwhelmed to speak. It was enough to have Bronco and Bob leaning from their saddles to hug her.

Finally, she began trying to answer their questions. It took several minutes to give them even the bare essentials of what had happened, and she could see the anger in Bronco's face when she finished. "I think we should go back and call the sheriff," he said. "That man must be caught and stopped before he manages to locate the treasure."

"He can't find it," Linda assured him, "not without the key from the sleigh."

"But he has the sleigh," Bob reminded her. "If he's as desperate as you say, he might just take an axe to it."

Linda opened her mouth to deny the suggestion, but she couldn't, for she remembered the cruel determination she'd seen in Gabe Ingram's face. Once he went to the cabin and discovered that she had escaped, she had no doubt that he would do exactly that. He'd have to know that she'd tell everything.

"We can stop him by taking the sleigh back to the stable," she said, the idea like a ray of hope.

"Where is it?" Bronco asked, then looked beyond her towards the sky. "We aren't going to have much time before the new storm hits, and I don't want to risk being somewhere on that trail. This is treacherous country—as you know all too well."

"It's in the cave I told you about," Linda replied. "The one where Randy and I took shelter."

"Can you find it?" Bob asked.

For a moment, her spirits drooped. Then she looked around. "We can follow the snowmobile tracks right to it," she said. "I remember coming out into that meadow when Mr Ingram was taking me to the cabin. If we start over there . . ." She touched her heels to Chica's sides and they raced across the snowy ground to the trees.

It took only a few minutes to find the track of the snowmobile, which was easy to follow in the sheltered area under the trees. As they rode along, Bob and Bronco described their terrible night as they'd waited for her return, sure that she'd been lost in the ground blizzard that had paralysed the whole area.

They'd instituted a small search last evening as soon as it stopped; but with only a short period of daylight, they'd had no luck at all. "I borrowed this horse last night," Bronco finished, "and Bob and I rode out to this valley as soon as it got light this morning. We figured this was the only place we could start, though we certainly didn't know what to expect."

"You shouldn't have come out here alone, Sis," Bob told her.

Linda sighed. "So I found out," she admitted. "But if it hadn't been for Randy . . ." She let her words trail off. "I do still owe him my life. If he hadn't taken me to the cave, I don't know what would have happened."

"Then he left you with that creep Ingram," Bob reminded her.

"There's the cave," Linda announced, peering ahead. "See it?"

"So what do we do now?" Bob asked. "Get the stuff and run?"

"I'd rather take the whole sleigh," Linda protested.

"How can we do that?" Bronco looked dubious.

"We've all got ropes on our saddles," Linda pointed out. "Why can't we pull it back? The trail is wide enough, and with three horses on different lengths of rope . . ."

Bronco sighed, his expression none too confident. But the rapidly greying sky kept him from discussing the idea further. "We'll try," he agreed, "but if it doesn't work, we'll have to abandon it and head for home. That storm isn't going to wait."

Linda nodded, well aware of the storm's potential after her experience in the ground blizzard. "It won't take long."

It took precious seconds to manoeuvre the sleigh out of the darkness of the cavern, but once the three ropes were tied to it, the handsome vehicle moved easily over the snow, hardly slowing their progress at all. Bronco's horse was given the longest rope, since he was less trained and more skittish. Rocket and Chica accepted the drag on their saddles without objection, Chica trotting along obediently with only a single rein to guide her.

The wind had quickened by the time they reached the ridge, and Linda was glad when the trail dropped down into the protection of the forest where the tall pines offered some relief from the icy cold. Still, she kept glancing at the sky, and she knew without being told that the race against the storm was going to be close.

Suddenly another sound rose above the steady howling of the wind: the rumble of a snowmobile motor! The riders stopped their horses. Linda was terrified that Gabe Ingram was coming to take the sleigh away once again.

One Last Try   14

The snowmobile came bouncing around a turn in
the trail and spluttered to a stop. For a moment,
Linda just sat still. Then her relief spilled over into
nearly hysterical laughter as Mr White came over to
her.

"Thank goodness you're safe," he said. "And
you've found the sleigh."

Linda could only nod.

"What are you doing out here, John?" Bronco
asked.

"I came after you. Give me your ropes and get
moving; I'll tow the sleigh in."

Bronco started to object, but their host was firm
and they had to yield, admitting that he was much
more able to find his way home through a storm.
Bob helped him secure the ropes to the sturdy
snowmobile; then the three of them urged their
weary horses into a lope, leaving Mr White alone
with the sleigh.

The first snowflakes were just beginning to swirl
around them as they rode into the stable yard.
Linda dismounted and dropped to her knees in the
snow when her legs refused to support her. Bob and
Bronco were beside her at once, and Doña and Mrs
White quickly came out along with the happy,
barking Rango.

"We'll take care of Chica," Bronco said. "You go
inside and get warm."

Linda was much too tired to argue. She was just grateful for the strong arms around her waist and the warm feeling of being loved and cared for that surrounded her as she was helped into the house.

By the time she'd had a hot bath and was wrapped securely in fresh clothes, there was a heaped plate of food waiting. John White came in while she was eating. He poured a cup of coffee and sat down opposite her. "Now," he said, "tell me everything."

"Start at the beginning," Bob ordered. "Why did you go out there in the first place, and what did you find?"

The story took over an hour to tell, with much of it having to be repeated and explained. When she got to the part about the journals that Mr Ingram had found, Mrs White gasped. "Melanie was in Australia? But how . . . why?"

"I guess we won't know that till the storm clears and we can get to the cabin to claim the journals," Linda answered. "I wanted to read them last night, but . . ."

Mr White broke in, frowning. "Do you suppose this Ingram is our mysterious claimant?"

Linda nodded. "He told Randy some story about being a descendant of Melanie Davis Howard, so I imagine he had someone put in the claim just to confuse us."

"Keep us too busy to figure out what he was really after," Bob agreed.

"I think we should call the sheriff," Mrs White said. "Randy will probably know where Ingram is hiding."

Linda squirmed in her chair, weighing her anger at Randy for abandoning Chica against her knowledge that she would have died in the ground blizzard without his help. "I don't think Randy really did anything bad," she said. "Mr Ingram lied to him, too."

Mrs White patted her shoulder. "Sheriff Hoskins can sort it all out," she assured her. "After all, he knows Randy and his family."

Linda pushed the empty plate away and sighed. "I feel human again," she announced. "It is so good to be back."

Doña laughed. "What would you like to do now, dear?" she asked. "Take a nap?"

Linda stood up and stretched. "I'd like to go to the stable," she said.

"Chica is just fine," Bob assured her. "I groomed her before I put her in her stall."

"Please," Linda insisted.

"The sleigh?" Bronco guessed.

Linda nodded.

Her grandfather's eyes told her that he understood her feelings. He moved to the window and peered out into the darkening afternoon. "Well, let's do it before the storm gets any worse," he agreed.

The stable was quiet and peaceful, and Linda smiled to see that the sleigh had been returned safely to its corner. She hesitated only a moment to whisper her thanks to Chica, then hurried over to show Bob and Bronco how the final compartment worked. The envelope, the sheet of journal, and the two black stones were still waiting where she'd left them.

Once back in the house, she presented the sheet and the envelope to Mrs White. "I didn't open this," she explained. "I thought that since it was addressed to your mother, you should be the one to do that."

Mrs White looked up at her and Linda could see the shining of tears in her eyes. "I only wish my mother was here to see all this," she said. "She mourned Melanie her whole life. She always felt that she could have done something to keep her here."

No one spoke as Mrs White gently lifted the flap of the envelope, breaking the seal. There was a single sheet inside, and Linda recognized the handwriting as Melanie's. The silence grew thick and heavy as tears filled Mrs White's eyes and spilled down her cheeks, unchecked. Finally, she simply handed the sheet to Linda. "You can read it to everyone," she whispered, then left the room.

"My dear Anne," the letter began.

Though I said farewell in my last journal sheet, I can't leave you without one more word. Our wedding was lovely, missing only your sweet presence at my side. I met Calvin in Sleeping Wells when he left his father and returned from Denver where they'd gone to a cattle show.

We spent our wedding night in the house that I dreamed would be ours, but now we must leave it and this valley, perhaps forever. Calvin says his father will never forgive me or him, so we will seek our fortune elsewhere.

I shall write to you again once the furore of my leaving has ebbed and, if Father can forgive me, perhaps we can hope to return. Till then, dear sister, know that I never willingly deceived you and that the keys to my love for you, and a part of me, will always be here with you in the sleigh and in our shared memories.

Your loving sister,

It was signed with a flourish, then beneath that was a more formal signature: *Melanie Davis*

Howard, Mrs Calvin Howard. Linda sighed and placed the old sheet of paper gently on the table. Silently she felt a surge of excitement. The word "key" had appeared again.

"Such a sad parting," Doña murmured. "They were obviously so close."

"I guess we won't find out why she went to Australia till we get the rest of the journals," Mr White said. "And that won't be till the storm clears and someone can get to the cabin."

Linda giggled. "I'll bet Mr Ingram was furious when he went there this morning," she mused. "Not only did I have a horse as an overnight guest, but I didn't even do last night's dishes."

"Gosh, he'll probably never invite you back," Bob teased.

The merry mood carried them through the rest of the day while the storm raged outside. The phone rang later in the evening while they were popping popcorn in the fireplace, and when John White returned from a long conversation, his face was grim.

"Some kind of trouble, John?" Bronco asked.

"Just frustrating," Mr White said, slumping down on the couch. "That was Sheriff Hoskins."

"Did they catch Ingram?" Bob asked.

"They haven't seen a sign of him," Mr White answered. "Hal said he talked to Randy for over an hour and the boy confessed to everything. It was pretty much what Linda told us, but he claims that he doesn't really know where Ingram might be hiding."

"Does Hal believe him?" Mrs White asked.

"Well, the boy did give him a room number at the hotel in Glacier Point where Ingram and another man were staying. Hal called, but the other man left yesterday and Ingram checked out early this morning." John White sounded disgusted.

Linda sighed. "He's probably at the cabin," she said. "He must have been sure that I'd tell him where the treasure was this morning, so he probably planned to just take it and run."

"If he's at the cabin, I doubt that he'll be foolish enough to try to go anywhere till the storm ends, and by then Hal will be waiting to catch him." John smiled.

"What is the sheriff going to do to Randy?" Linda asked.

Mr White shrugged. "I doubt that he'll do anything unless we press charges, and I don't have any desire to do that. Do you, Beatrice?"

Mrs White shook her head. "I think it should be up to Linda," she said. "She's the only one who has actually been injured in all this."

"That really wasn't Randy's fault," Linda admitted. "I wouldn't want to have him get into serious trouble. After all, he did save my life when the ground blizzard came up."

"I think the best thing would be a prolonged probation," Bronco observed. "Something to make him aware of just how serious this all was, but not severe enough to ruin his life, since he does have the potential to grow into a decent young man."

John White nodded. "That's approximately what I suggested to Hal," he said. "I think he will try and use his influence to make sure he receives fair treatment."

"Anyone for popcorn?" Bob asked, opening the popper and allowing the snowy kernels to spill over into the big bowl that Mrs White had provided. "Fresh, hot popcorn."

They went to bed early, everyone exhausted from the worry and fear that had haunted them all the night before when Linda had been missing and alone. Linda slept easily and without dreams, lulled by the steady wail of the wind as it drove the snow against the building.

It was perhaps the silence that woke her, and she sat up, startled. The illuminated dial of her bedside clock informed her that it was nearly six-thirty. Though she knew that the sun wouldn't be up yet, she slipped out of bed and padded barefoot and shivering to the window.

The frost and mounded snow left her little viewing space, but after a moment of scraping she peered out at a world of white stillness. Snow and wind had stopped and left behind a fantasyland of light and shadow. The trees and the area beneath them were total darkness, and the snow that feathered the heavy pine limbs and covered the ground was pure and untouched as yet, making a world that looked brand-new.

Linda stared at the scene till her icy feet forced her back to the warmth of her bed. Once there, however, she had no desire to sleep, for now her mind was busy with what lay ahead. After breakfast she had every intention of going to the valley to retrieve the treasure. Today was the day that they would finally find out what Melanie had hidden so many years ago.

At the first sound of movement within the house, she was up and dressing, the entries from the journals running through her mind, the final odd-shaped stone clutched in her hand as she puzzled over it. She carried it with her when she went to breakfast.

"What's up?" she asked when she reached the table and found that everyone was looking her way questioningly.

"Sheriff Hoskins just called and said that he'd be over sometime this morning," Mrs White informed her. "He has all sorts of information about this man Ingram and his illegal activities on the West Coast."

Linda laughed, helping herself to the stack of pancakes, then adding a mound of golden scrambled eggs. "That doesn't surprise me," she admitted. "Does that mean you'll have to stay here all morning?"

"I'm afraid so," Mrs White said.

"What about the treasure?" Linda asked.

"What about it?" Mrs White inquired, and Linda could see the concern in all the faces turned her way.

"I think we should go after it now," she answered them. "I mean, Randy probably told Ingram where he found me and Ingram might go looking there himself. It's always possible that he could dig up the floor and find it even without the key."

"Do you really think that's possible?" Doña asked.

"He is a terribly determined man," Linda replied.

"Are you saying you want to go after it yourself?" Bronco asked, his eyes twinkling.

Linda nodded.

"We wouldn't be able to go with you this early," Mr White warned. "And you'll have to ride your horses—my friend came to get his snowmobile first thing this morning. He uses it to go to work when the roads haven't been ploughed."

"I won't be able to go with you, either," Bronco said. "My horse threw a shoe on the way home last night. He was limping by the time we reached the stable."

145

"Bob and I can handle it," Linda assured them, her gaze on her brother. "Right?"

"I can hardly wait," he responded, eagerly.

"You'll be careful?" Doña murmured. "After that storm . . ."

"We'll be very careful," Bob and Linda chorused, eating as quickly as they could.

"Just don't worry if you can't find it," Mrs White said. "Knowing so much about Melanie and about my own mother's early life here is treasure enough for me."

"You just make sure the sheriff nabs old Ingram," Linda told her. "We'll find the treasure; Melanie left good instructions."

In spite of their eagerness, it was well over an hour before the horses were saddled and ready. They rode away to a chorus of shouted good wishes from those remaining behind. The air was sharp and cold, but the bright sun made it seem warmer.

"So do you really know where the treasure is, Linda?" Bob asked as they hurried along the now familiar trail to the secluded valley, the horses gently fighting their firm hold on the reins.

"I think I can find it," Linda said confidently. "I mean, I don't know exactly where it is, but I did find the house foundation, and we have the last key."

"I just hope we're in time," Bob said.

Linda grinned at him. "I don't think there is any way Mr Ingram could find the treasure without the stone," she admitted.

"But you said . . ." Bob began, then he chuckled.

"Did you want to sit around the house all day and wait for the sheriff?" Linda asked.

He shook his head. "All I can say is, you'd better find that treasure."

They rode on in silence, not stopping till they reached the ridge above the valley. Bob surveyed the scene. "So where is the house?" he asked.

"The foundation is just to the left of those big pines and about fifty yards from the stream," Linda answered, pointing towards the area.

"Well, we're obviously the first ones here since the storm," Bob said.

Linda nodded, her eyes taking in the unbroken vistas of wind-rippled snow. "So let's go down and get to work," she suggested.

"Lead the way."

Linda located the foundation again without difficulty, and Bob quickly shovelled the snow off the stones that formed the floor between the tumbled walls. As he worked, Linda backed away from the ruined house, holding the final stone carefully.

"So, have you figured out what the marks on it mean?" Bob asked, leaning on his shovel handle.

"It's the house all right," Linda answered, "and the little x could be right over in this area." Linda pointed towards a pile of stones that were jutting out slightly from beneath a pile of snow.

"I don't know, let's see."

Bob began scraping the snow from the fragile pile of stones his sister was referring to. "This looks like it could be the remains of a fireplace," he muttered to himself as he worked. He finished scooping the accumulated snow out of the way, then cleared leaves, pine needles, and other debris from the spot. "So what are we looking for?" he asked.

"The keyhole for this stone key," Linda said, kneeling on the damp, cold stones and running her gloved fingers carefully along the edges of each uncovered stone.

Bob joined her, their concentration so riveted on what they were doing that neither of them heard the distant sound of a motor throbbing. Suddenly Linda's gloved finger slipped down between two of the stones. She gasped.

"What is it?" Bob asked.

"It could be a keyhole," Linda replied, her hands shaking so much she had a hard time fitting the small black stone into the spot. Very carefully, she tried turning it like a key—and to her utter amazement, the stone began to lift.

"You did it, Sis!" Bob bent to help her, easing the hollowed stone back to explore the carefully constructed hole beneath it. A metal strongbox lay there, dull and dusty in the light of the warming sun.

Linda's hands were trembling as she lifted the box out of the hole, and Bob let the heavy stone drop back into place, handing her the black stone key. They got to their feet at the same time and Linda let him take the box.

He turned it over in his hands carefully. "It's locked," he informed her. "We'll . . ."

Linda had turned away from him, her ears suddenly tuned to the approaching roar of a motor. As she watched, a familiar yellow snowmobile broke out of the trees and came racing across the fresh snow in their direction.

"It's him!" she gasped. "Bob, it's Ingram!"

"Let's get out of here," Bob shouted, already heading for Rocket.

Linda raced towards Chica, but even as she caught the filly's trailing reins, she knew it was too late. The snowmobile shot by her, headed for Bob with deadly accuracy. Linda screamed as the machine swerved at the last moment, grazing Bob and knocking him into the snow as Gabe Ingram snatched the strongbox from his hands.

"Bob?" She took a step in his direction.

"Go after him," Bob shouted at her. "Don't let him get away with the treasure."

Seeing that he was already scrambling to his feet and reaching for his reins, Linda vaulted to Chica's back and urged the willing filly forward after the speeding snowmobile. For the first half-dozen bounds, they were gaining on the machine, but then Ingram settled down and headed away from her at high speed, too fast for the game but already tiring filly.

Linda glanced around, aware that the deep snow was slowing Chica. The snow in the forest area was much lighter and she could see that Ingram would have to pass close to the belt of trees if he continued on his present course. Knowing that it was her only chance, she guided Chica away from the snowmobile, ducking low so that her head and shoulders were alongside the filly's neck as they left the glowing sunlight for the shadowy forest.

One quick look back at the house foundation showed her that Bob was now mounted on Rocket and racing after the snowmobile, his lariat in his hand as though he'd read her mind. Linda clung to the saddlehorn to keep her balance as the filly dodged between the pines and under the protective canopy of their spreading limbs.

"Go, Chica, go," Linda urged. "We can't let him have it. We just can't. Let's head him off."

The filly responded with a burst of speed that truly amazed Linda, especially as she leaped a fallen tree and swirled through a drift in a small gully. There was no need to guide her, only to hang on and hope that no trap hid beneath the fluffy blanket to catch her flying hooves.

A low-hanging branch slashed at Linda's face,

Chica dodged between the pines . . .

scraping her cheek and half blinding her, but she held on, burying her face against the straining muscles in the filly's neck.

Over the sounds of their passage, she could hear the roar of the snowmobile. She turned to peer between the trees and saw that thanks to Chica's blazing speed they were now even with the machine, which had been slowed by the hidden roughness of the area that Ingram was crossing.

As she watched, the snowmobile struck something under the snow and lurched dangerously, nearly spilling Ingram out. He slowed even further, heading in her direction to keep away from Bob and Rocket, who were also being slowed by the drifts of snow the wind had left in the uneven field.

Linda guided Chica towards the end of the trees, bursting clear of them just as the snowmobile approached. Ingram opened his mouth to shout at her, jerking the machine around to avoid crashing into the now weary filly. As he did so, Bob's rope snaked out and the perfect loop settled over the man's head and shoulders. With his arms pinned to his sides, he was jerked off the seat of the machine.

The snowmobile shot away from him, then sputtered to a halt against the sturdy trunk of the nearest tree. Bob was on the ground tying Ingram's hands behind him even before Linda dismounted to pick up the strongbox, which appeared uninjured from being pitched into the snow.

"Going somewhere, Mr Ingram?" she inquired politely.

"What do you think you're doing?" Ingram demanded, his face dark with fury.

"Well, if your snowmobile is all right, we're taking you back to the Whites' to talk to Sheriff Hoskins," Bob said calmly. "If it isn't running, we may be taking you for a little horseback ride." He grinned at Linda, handing her the end of his rope. "Hang on to him while I check the machine."

"I knew you could find the treasure," Ingram growled.

Linda smiled at him sweetly. "All you needed was the right key to open everything up," she agreed, then looked around at the roar of the snowmobile motor. Bob rode it back to them.

"If we had the time, I think I'd make you walk," Bob told him. "But I'm very anxious to find out what we have in that strongbox, and I think the sheriff is looking for you, so . . ." He shrugged. "Get on and behave yourself or I swear I'll just leave you."

Linda mounted the filly and collected Rocket's reins. "You go on ahead with him," she told Bob. "I'll take it easy on the horses."

"You keep the box," Bob said. "No use tempting Mr Ingram."

"But . . ." Linda began, then nodded, under-standing his reasoning. "Be careful," she called after him as he guided the snowmobile back the way he'd come.

The ride to the Whites' seemed to take forever. She was conscious every minute of the weight of the strongbox, her mind whirling with the possibilities of what it might contain. She was very glad when she finally left the trees and rode into the Whites' stable yard.

Bob and Bronco were waiting to take the horses, ordering her to go inside the house at once. Linda obeyed, carrying the strongbox in shaking hands.

Once inside, she placed it in Mrs White's lap. "We didn't find a key," she said, "but this must be the treasure box."

"Let me see it," Sheriff Hoskins volunteered, coming to look at the box. "I just might be able to spring the lock for you."

Linda looked around. "Where is Mr Ingram?" she asked.

"On his way to jail," the sheriff answered. "My deputy picked him up about fifteen minutes ago."

Linda shook back her hair and sank down at the table, watching as the sheriff worked expertly on the lock. It was several minutes before they all heard the faint click. The sheriff opened the catch, but handed the strongbox back to Mrs White without opening it. At that same moment, Bronco and Bob came in.

"So what did we find?" Bob asked breathlessly.

"That is what we are about to learn," Mrs White said, lifting the lid.

The room was still except for a chorus of soft gasps as Mrs White lifted a piece of black velvet and exposed the contents of the box. It was a crèche, each figure carefully and lovingly carved of dark wood, then heavily inlaid with thin sheets of gold and set with precious gems.

Mary's gown was touched with sapphires; Joseph's robe with a belt of emeralds; the Christ Child was crowned with the flashing fire of diamonds. The Three Wise Men glittered with many jewels, and even the camels and the lowly donkey were touched with gold. It was the most incredibly beautiful display Linda had ever seen.

Mrs White set the delicate figures out carefully, her fingers reverent, and Linda could see that, even without the gold and jewels, they would have commanded attention for the perfection of the carving. "It truly is a treasure," she whispered.

"And one that everyone can see and enjoy, thanks to you," Mrs White told her through her tears.

No one else spoke for several minutes, then Sheriff Hoskins sighed. "I'm afraid I'll need a statement from you, Linda," he said. "Something we can use when we charge Ingram for all his crimes."

"My pleasure," Linda told him, remembering the casual way he'd dismissed Chica's plight and had left her alone in the cabin that stormy night.

The next two days flew by as they prepared for a belated New Year's celebration. Linda was dizzy with excitement that final evening as she slipped into her best dress. It was a soft, glowing deep red wool that made the most of her dark hair and eyes and gave an extra blush of colour to her cheeks. A tap on the door interrupted and she quickly invited Doña and Mrs White to come in.

"Almost ready for the party?" Mrs White asked.

Linda nodded. "I'm really looking forward to it," she said, "except that I hate to think that this is our last night here. I'll never forget everything that's happened."

"And we won't forget it either," Mrs White assured her.

"You'll have to let us know what you hear from your Australian relations," Doña told her friend. "I'm sure they will be very interested to know about Melanie's family here."

"I'm just glad that she had a good and happy life there," Mrs White murmured. "Her journals are all so full of joy. Her only sadness was never knowing what happened to her family in the States."

Linda nodded. "Her letters must have been lost somewhere between Australia and here. She probably just decided that no one wanted to write to her."

"Before we go out to the stable to join all our guests, there is something I want to give you, Linda," Mrs White said.

"Oh, I don't . . ." Linda began, then gasped as she recognized Mrs White's gold chain in her outstretched hand.

"I hope you like it, dear," Mrs White went on, smiling, "and that you'll think of us whenever you wear it."

"I'll never forget any of you," Linda assured her, "and this is lovely."

"May I put it on for you?" Doña asked.

Linda nodded, touching the series of golden beads that now separated the three black stones, spacing them perfectly with the key in the middle to form a very different, but quite elegant necklace. The black and gold showed beautifully against the ruby wool, and when she peeked in the mirror, Linda saw that she appeared as happy as she felt.

"Now, let's go and greet this New Year properly," Mrs White said, "with friends."

Laughing, the three went out to the stable, which had been cleaned and decorated. There the priceless crèche now rested on display beside the sleigh that had kept its secret through the years. Music filled the air, carrying a tide of laughter and conversation as the Saddle Club members and the Whites' other friends danced or wandered from refreshment table to stall doors to pat Chica and Rocket, who were also honoured guests.

Linda went to pet her horse, then touched the black stones of the necklace, smiling. In spite of all the frightening things that had happened, it had been a wonderful vacation and she was sorry that she had to leave. Still, she knew that more adventures awaited her.

"Dance, Linda?" Allen asked. She left Chica with a final pat. It would be a Happy New Year, she was sure.

SUPERSLEUTHS

by FRANKLIN W. DIXON and CAROLYN KEENE

A feast of reading for all mystery fans!

At last, the Hardy Boys and Nancy Drew have joined forces to become the world's most brilliant detective team!

Together, the daredevil sleuths investigate seven spine-chilling mysteries: a deadly roller-coaster that hurtles to disaster, a sinister bell that tolls in a city of skeletons, a haunted opera house with a sinister curse — and many more terrifying situations.

Nancy Drew and the Hardy Boys — *dynamite!*

Armada

The Nancy Drew Mystery Stories®
by Carolyn Keene

Have you read all the titles in this thrilling series?

The Quest of the Missing Map (6)

Nancy's search for buried treasure takes her to exotic Little Palm Island. But someone is desperate to find the hoard before her . . .

The Ghost of Blackwood Hall (11)

Blood-curdling danger awaits Nancy when she investigates a mansion haunted by a terrifying phantom . . .

The Swami's Ring (55)

Eastern mysticism and mystery go hand in hand for Nancy when she searches for a stolen ring — fabulous jewel of the maharajahs. But deep in the woods a deadly snake lies in wait for her . . .

The Twin Dilemma (57)

When a glamorous New York model disappears, Nancy steps in to take her place. But the glittering world of fashion hides an ugly secret . . .

Armada